The Dancer

The Dancer 2023, Originally published as a Storytel Original Series

Corylus Books Ltd

corylusbooks.com

ISBN: 978-1-7392989-5-1

The Dancer

Óskar Guðmundsson

Translated by Quentin Bates

Published by Corylus Books Ltd

THE DANCER

1

The early hours, Monday, 6th December 1982

He switched on the wipers. They whined like a beaten dog as they cleared the snow piled up on the windscreen. It was a pitch-black night, without a breath of wind, and larger-than-usual snowflakes fluttered like feathers to the ground.

There must be millions of them, he thought. Most likely billions. He sat behind the wheel of the stationary van and stared out through the windscreen, looking out into the blackness. He started and glanced quickly in the wing mirror, certain that he had seen something. It was just the smoke of the vehicle's own exhaust. It was red as it curled upwards, illuminated in the glow of the brake lights. It was almost similar to the vapour he was aware of coming from his open mouth when he breathed fast, lit up by the yellow dashboard lights. A low mutter came from the engine. Normally, he liked to hear it purr. But not tonight. Now it sounded like a growling predator about to launch an attack. He could feel soreness as he rubbed his index finger against his thumb. He looked down at the dark patch that had formed where the leather needle had pierced the flesh of his index finger. He held his hand close to his face. He sniffed and closed his eyes as he took in the aroma of the leather polish. He recalled the previous night, working the polish deep into the leather with his fingers.

He opened his eyes and flicked on the headlights, illuminating the snow-covered area ahead of the van. That and the victim who sat tied to a chair, his back to him, struggling against his bonds. He switched the lights to full beam, so that he could see clearly the thick, dark leather mask that covered the victim's head. He gripped the wheel with both hands and leaned close to the windscreen. He found himself fascinated by the sparkling light reflected from the snowflakes around the four taut chains hooked into iron rings fixed high on the mask. He was delighted with what he had achieved in designing it. There were chains on each side of the mask, running diagonally down to the frozen ground where they were fastened securely with tent pegs. The same went for the chain fixed to the centre of the mask's forehead. The fourth chain was snapped onto a ring at the back of the mask's neck and ran horizontally to the top of a metre-high iron fence post hammered into the ground behind the chair. He watched as one chain was pulled taut as another lay slack, depending on how hard the victim fought.

The man picked up a sledge hammer from the passenger side footwell and got out of the van. He went over to the iron post and after adjusting it a little to one side, he took the hammer in both hands, raised it high and dropped six heavy blows. Then he tested the post and seemed to be satisfied that it was secure. The victim in the chair did his best to look behind him.

'What are you doing? You don't need to do this. You must forgive me. I...'

The victim got no further as the man pulled at one of the chains, jerking his head. For a moment he looked into the victim's terrified eyes, inside small openings in the mask.

'Yeah. I ought to,' the man said in a low voice.

He went to the van, slid open the side door and switched on a small light inside. He put the sledgehammer on the floor inside the van and slowly removed his clothes. When they had been neatly folded, he reached for a bulky Marantz tape player and placed it on the van's bonnet. He didn't feel the cold that nipped at his naked body. On the contrary, he felt an inner heat thanks to the adrenaline flooding through him, boosting his heartbeat. He relished the feeling of it rushing through his body, knowing that it both stifled and dispelled the fear that lurked deep inside. If the fear were to gain the upper hand, then his veins would tighten, and he would lose his nerve. There could be no question of backing out now. He couldn't back out, no way.

The man's hands rested on the bonnet on each side of the player. He lowered his head, eyes closed. There was silence, except for the moans of the victim in the chair. These seemed to be carried from deep in the belly of his surroundings. Nobody would hear those cries. He opened his eyes. For a moment he stared at the tape player. With one quick movement, he pressed the play button.

Loud, hard, rhythmic music burst from the speakers.

The man straightened his back and took a deep breath. He turned, stepping quickly towards the victim, and danced as if in a trance.

He swayed, strutted and jerked his body, his belly pulsing so that his ribs stood proud, and his head swooped here and there. Just before the vocals broke in, he approached the chair, placing his face close to his victim's, staring into the openings in the mask.

His voice was shrill as he sang.

I'm not your slave

The man danced circles around the victim, twisting as he leaped over the diagonal chains, and limboing under or leaping over the horizontal chain behind him. He danced ring after ring around him, playing at stepping occasionally onto chains fastened to the floor, the victim moaning in pain every time his head jerked. The dancer moved further from the victim, who squinted into the gloom as he left the area illuminated by the van's lights. All the same, he could see his indistinct outline as he danced as though possessed, kicking snow high into the air around him. Then he vanished as the darkness swallowed him. The victim breathed harder than ever as the music pounded in his ears.

Not your slave Not your slave Not your slave

The victim's eyes stared out into the blackness as he held his breath. It was as if time stood still, jerked back into action as a scream grew in intensity. The dancer's dark silhouette leaped out of the darkness towards him. He danced a few more circles around the victim, crouched down, and leaped like a high jumper to land with his full weight on the horizontal chain, snapping the victim's head back. The tent peg securing the chain in front of the victim shot out of the ground. If it hadn't been for the music, the dancer would have heard the crack of the victim's neck snapping.

The dancer rolled over onto his front, plunging his face into the snow. After a moment's motionlessness, he jumped to his feet and ran to the car. He switched off the player.

The silence of the heath screamed at him.

THE DANCER

2

Friday 3rd December 1982, three days prior

Old Jón opened the workshop's doors. It was small and cramped, and the ceiling was unusually high, which made the workshop feel more spacious than it really was. There were two tall windows in one wall, and if they had been cleaner, then maybe they would have let in more light. A variety of wooden boards, planks and cardboard boxes were piled in stacks that rested on rafters beneath the pitched roof. The air was heavy with sawdust and wood oil.

Jón's workshop was one of the few of its kind left in the centre of the city. Larger and more efficient places had opened up, picking up the larger contracts. Jón had previously had a workshop down by Skúlagata, and back then he had hardly been able to keep up with the demand for the popular sideboards and living room cabinets that Jón had designed and sold to practically every other household in the country. But the arrival of a Swedish furniture and fittings giant a year ago had resulted in Jón's trade being seriously diminished, and he had moved to this little place on Vitastígur. He handled repairs and suchlike maintenance for smaller companies and individuals who generally took advantage of this good-natured man, getting away with paying far too little, often late, or not at all. All the same, Jón had always paid his grandson Tony the proper rate during the three years he had worked for him. There were times when Tony hadn't written down all his hours and had even offered to hand in his notice. Jón wouldn't hear of it, and often slipped him a banknote or two between paydays. *Take some nice girl out for a hot dog and an ice cream*, he usually suggested as he handed over a little extra.

'Not heading home yet, Tony?' he said from the doorway, peering at the clock on the wall, which showed it was getting on for six.

'No, I wanted to finish this,' Tony said when he had switched off the lathe and taken off his safety glasses.

'All right. It's fine to pack it in now. We don't have to deliver this job until next week,' he said, taking a box of snuff from his pocket. He tapped a respectable mound of powder onto the back of his hand, and it vanished into both of his nostrils in a single fluid movement, after which he put his hand to his heart. 'This is going to finish me off one day. You don't want any more, do you?' he continued, hanging his coat on a nail by the door.

Tony shook his head.

'That's just as well,' Jón said and adjusted the braces that held up his generously sized jeans. He looked into the grimy mirror that hung next to his coat, took a comb from his breast pocket and ran it through his straggling grey beard. There was no need to put the comb anywhere near his hair-free head. 'Tony, I've been thinking.'

'About what?'

'Don't you want to get on with the cabinet making apprenticeship? You'd already finished one term, and there's every chance you'd be able to have your work here assessed towards it,' he said, trying to sound encouraging.

'I'm not sure.'

'I'd be happy to support you through it. I can put a few payments towards the course. And I could help out with your mother as well.'

Tony didn't reply.

'It'd be a good start for you. You could even take over this place and build it up.'

Tony showed no response.

'All right, my boy. How's the new flat? Have you painted it yet?'

'Old,' he said.

'Who's old?' he asked in surprise.

'The flat's old. And it's only the extension out the back that I'm renting from her.'

'Her?'

'The woman. It's an elderly woman who owns the house and she lives there,' Tony said as he swept sawdust from beneath the lathe.

'Well... Doesn't she have nice legs?' his grandfather asked with a laugh.

Tony didn't respond, used to these unsophisticated remarks about women. All the same, he couldn't help smiling inwardly as he saw his grandfather laugh, as it seemed that every sinew in his face revelled in the joke. His ears lifted, his eyes glittered and the lines around them deepened. Tony almost expected him to slap his own thigh, but it didn't happen this time.

'Don't you need to paint the place? I can give you a hand with that,' he continued.

'I've already painted everything, but thanks all the same,' Tony said, and undid the band that held back his long, dark hair.

'So who looks after your mother? I mean, when you've moved.'

'I go and see her regularly. And there's a lady who comes three times a week to help her,' he said quickly, as he saw his grandfather's mouth open, maybe ready to make another suggestion. He took care to turn away as he had got to know his grandfather's uncanny talent for divining from his expression whether or not he was being told the truth.

'Well, that's good. So how is my daughter these days?'

'Mum's fine,' Tony replied as he took off his overalls, hanging them on a nail next to his grandfather's coat. 'Sometimes she forgets to eat, and to take her medication.'

'I ought to go and see her. I haven't seen her for... Ach. I don't remember when it was, last Christmas, probably. Or was it the Christmas before? It's not good enough. Your mother's a good woman...' he muttered absently, and hesitated. 'Listen, it looks like I've wrecked the old banger on the corner,' he said, sitting up straight in his chair once the awkward silence had hung in the air a little too long.

Tony sighed discreetly, relieved that he had changed the subject.

'Which corner?'

'Well, just up the street,' Jón said, and paused to energetically blow his nose into a handkerchief. 'Where Lindargata meets Vitastígur,' he continued, taking a seat at the shabby, ancient desk that some customer had never got round to collecting, and which now served as the workshop's coffee table. 'There's a pile of ice and it ripped off something from underneath. Either the city council's piggy bank is empty, or they simply can't be bothered to keep the city's streets clear. Maybe it's just as well, because the doctor told me just the other day that I need to be more active, so it won't do me any harm to walk to work and back home again. Coffee?' he asked, offering a cup to Tony, who again shook his head. 'What's the matter with you, my lad? Aren't you ever going to grow up? I reckon you're the only twenty-year-old there is who hasn't got a taste for coffee yet,' he said cheerfully.

'Do you want me to go and sort it out?' Tony asked, tying his hair back again.

'Sort what out?'

'The van.'

'That wouldn't go amiss, if it's not too much trouble,' he said, placing the keys on the table. 'And you could fix it up as well. It shouldn't be that much of a problem to bodge the exhaust together, but remember that third gear doesn't work at all. Sure you don't want me to come with you? Help with the painting?'

'Thanks, but no,' Tony said with a smile. He didn't have the heart to remind him that he had only just told him that the job was already done. 'I need to drop in and see Mum on the way,' he said, picking up the keys from the desk.

Jón mumbled something as he turned the white coffee mug in his hands and Tony heard him mutter to himself.

Ought to go and see her.

'I'd leave that for a while,' Tony said.

'Leave what?' he asked, looking up in surprise at Tony, who had pulled on a padded brown corduroy jacket.

'Going to see Mum. She doesn't want to see anyone these days. See you in the morning.'

3

The weather was rapidly worsening and sharp gusts of wind sent flurries of snow in every direction between the houses along Laugavegur. People on the street pulled their collars close, leaned into the wind and walked faster. Those who weren't dressed for the weather found themselves pointless errands to run so they could shelter in shops.

Tony mulled over what his grandfather had said concerning his mother, which he felt was out of kilter with reality, as the truth was that his mother wanted nothing whatsoever to do with his grandfather. He tried to embrace the idea that his grandfather's meaning had been that everyone is good during the first years of life, but for some reason we tend to lose those qualities somewhere along the way. As far as Tony could remember, his grandfather had done everything in his power to help his daughter through her difficulties and illnesses. But she wouldn't accept any kind of help. He had also tried to help Tony and even tried to rescue him. When things at home had been at their worst, with the drinking and the chaos, he had offered to take Tony. He could still remember the screams and abuse when she threw Jón out.

Tony had occasionally asked his grandfather about his mother's behaviour towards him, but there had never been many answers. His mother had said a few times that her father hadn't been there to save her when she had most needed him. On the other hand, she had always been drunk or in a bad way whenever she mentioned this. All the same, Tony knew perfectly well that her behaviour over the years had been such that Jón would have had every right to exclude her from his life. He knew that this was difficult when a family member was concerned. The thought had more than once occurred to him that he should disown her as his mother.

He stamped his feet, blew on his palms, and dusted the snow from his long dark hair as he walked into the Vísir supermarket on Laugavegur.

'Don't get snow on anything, please, love?' the middle-aged woman in the shop amiably admonished. 'This lot wasn't on the forecast,' she continued as she price-stamped goods by the cash register.

Tony went deeper into the narrow shop, where the choice of goods was remarkably broad, considering how small the place was. He checked out the sandwiches that were made on the premises, wondering at the same time if he was actually hungry. He heard a burst of laughter and noticed a girl and two lads who looked to be around his own age. He watched the lad slide a packet of biscuits inside his blue Millet down anorak.

'What are you up to?' the girl hissed. 'Put it back,' she added, glancing at Tony, who pretended to have seen nothing.

'Take it easy,' the lad said.

'We're hungry,' the other boy said with a grin.

'Now. Put it back or I'm going.'

'Calm down,' he said, putting the biscuits back on the shelf. 'If you really want biscuits that badly, then I'll buy them,' she said, eyes again flickering in Tony's direction. Their eyes met and they exchanged a smile. 'Come on, we need to get to the theatre. We're going to be late,' she continued. 'Really not looking forward to this dance practice tonight.'

'Hey, it'll be great. We get to practise on the main stage,' the lad in the Millet coat said.

Tony watched them make for the door. He noticed how the girl's feet splayed outwards as she tripped lightly towards the exit. He also noticed the lad in the Millet coat pick up a bag of doughnuts from the display by the door. The bell above the door tinkled as they opened it and went outside.

'See you again,' the cashier said to their disappearing backs.

Tony thought for a moment, then followed them out, lengthening his stride as he saw them disappear round the corner of Traðarkotssund.

'Hey,' he called out to them.

They turned.

'Hæ,' the girl said.

Tony stood still in silence. They stood as if they had been frozen to the ground. 'Want a doughnut?' the Millet coat guy asked.

'You're such an arsehole,' the girl said, slapping his shoulder.

'Are you after something?' she asked, catching Tony's eye. 'No, well... I heard you say something about a dance practice. I saw a small ad the other day about the dance troupe looking for more guys to join up.'

'Yes, but nobody's replied to the ad, as far as I know. Do you dance?'

'Yeah... a bit,' he said after a pause.

'It's a ballet class,' said the boy who had been mostly quiet up to now, shivering as the chill got to him.

'I know,' Tony replied in a low voice.

'We have to get moving. The old witch will haul us over the coals if we're late for the meeting. You're welcome to come with us,' the girl said as they turned and headed towards the National Theatre.

'What do you think he's going to get out of a meeting?' the Millet coat lad said. 'Just come to the practice this evening,' he said, and blinked.

'Yeah, sure,' the girl agreed. 'Practice starts at seven and we'll be on the main stage. Hey, what did you say your name is?'

'Tony.'

'OK. That's Davíð,' she said, indicating her companion in the Millet coat. 'And that's Oddur. My name's Hulda. Go in through the National Theatre main entrance and head into the auditorium,' she said as they set off.

'Looking forward to seeing you at the practice,' Oddur called over his shoulder to Tony, waving and fluttering his fingers like a pianist.

4

Tony had to watch every step along Öldugata. Ice on the streets had made life a misery for pedestrians for the last month and the letters pages of the newspapers carried endless furious complaints from people who had broken bones due to the city authorities' failure to act.

He reached the handsome two-storey house where his mother lived without having an accident on the way. The black cat sat by the front door. It rubbed itself against Tony's legs and shot in through the opening as soon as he opened the door.

'Is that you?' called a feeble voice from the bedroom further along the narrow, gloomy corridor, as he came in.

The house was dark and he watched the cat as it trotted to the kitchen. He peered into the spacious living room, where the glow from the street lights right outside made its way in through yellowing curtains that had once been as white as snow. The living room floor was empty, as the sofa, table and chairs had been placed by the walls around the room. A large teak board leaned against one wall. The weak light played across the discoloured parquet floor, darker towards the centre. The green Persian carpet that had been there for many years was now rolled up and lay across the three-seater sofa. The only piece of furniture that now seemed to be in use was a little circular coffee table that occupied a space in one corner. The lamp that stood on it was made of marble, and its curry-yellow lampshade, which had once been frilled, lolled sideways as if tired of playing its part. Four faded embroidered pictures hung on the walls, along with a handful of paintings. The largest of these was a watercolour that had at one time been protected by a sheet of glass, but this had been broken years ago.

Anyone troubling to take a closer look would have been able to locate a shard of the coffee set, painted with birds, lodged between the picture and the frame. A depression in the picture's surface could also be identified, and this was where a cup from the coffee set had collided with the glass, shattering both.

Tony went into the kitchen where the cat sat in front of an empty bowl and eyed him with an expectant look. He opened the fridge and poured milk into the bowl.

Despite the dirty crockery on the kitchen table and in the sink, the smell of detergent was overpowering. He no longer noticed it, any more than he noticed the fast, rhythmic drip of the kitchen tap. Without looking, he pressed the light switch and the fluorescent lights under the cupboards flickered and settled into a steady brightness.

'Is that you, Tony?' the voice asked, a little stronger this time.

Tony squatted and looked at the floor. He passed one hand over the brown-patterned tiles. Then he got to his feet and switched on the light that hung over the kitchen table, before going down on his knees. He again ran a hand over the tiles, leaned in close and felt along the floor as if looking for grains of sand. He quickly stood up, took a cloth from the sink and reached for the torch kept on a shelf above the fridge. He lay on the floor, on his back. Switching on the torch, he directed the beam of light upwards, under the front of the kitchen cupboards, pushing with his feet as he felt along the edge of the base of the cupboards. He noticed three tiny smudges, and vigorously wiped them with the cloth until they had disappeared.

'Tony, answer me. Who's out there?' the voice called, cracking like a needle on a scratched record.

He stood up and stared at the cloth, then threw it into the sink. He stood for a moment in thought, his gaze on the sink. He noticed that the rhythm of dripping water had stopped, as the drops now hit the cloth.

Tony opened the fridge and took out a saucepan of stew that he placed on one of the hot plates. He switched the stove on and stirred the stew with a wooden spoon. He opened the cupboard above the oven and took out three bottles of pills. When he had selected three tablets and placed them on the kitchen table, he used the base of an empty coke bottle to crush them. He swept the powder into a glass he had filled with orange juice. The white powder floated on the surface of the juice and disappeared into the liquid as he stirred it vigorously with one finger.

'Of course it's me,' he said in a low voice as he went into the bedroom where his mother lay in a single bed under the window. 'You shouldn't close the window all the way. You can hardly breathe in here.'

'You don't want me to freeze to death, do you?' she demanded.

'No, I don't want you to die of cold. You'll never die, Mum,' he said, still in the same low voice.

'What's that?'

'Nothing,' he said, giving her a broad smile as he put a hand behind her to support her head, and despite her attempt to avoid the glass, the contents finally went down her throat. He put his hands under her arms, lifting her to sit upright. He took in her grey, thin face with its hollow cheeks. Her yellowish hair was pushed back, except at the back of her head where she had lain on it.

'Come on, then. Let's get ourselves something to eat,' he said, helping her into the wheelchair. The wheels squeaked as he pushed it in front of him.

'It'd make a change to have something other than this

lousy stew day after day,' she said as they sat at the kitchen table.

'It's a perfectly good stew,' Tony said, feeding his mother a spoonful of meat and potato, before wiping away a trickle of gravy that ran down her cheek. 'I'll make something else tomorrow. This is the last of it.'

'You reckon I don't know what it'll be? Another meat stew with some other meat that'll last the whole week long. Maybe even the week after next as well. You're such an arsehole...'

If the medication hadn't left her so muddled and weak, she would have flinched as Tony suddenly banged the table with his clenched fist.

He stood up, threw his plate into the sink, jerked the wheelchair and pushed it into the living room where he parked it next to the round table. He adjusted the shade and switched on the lamp. He didn't notice when the shade drooped back to its former position.

He opened the heavy wooden sideboard that stood against one wall and took out a bottle of vodka and a glass, placing them on the table and half-filling the glass.

'I don't want to drink,' his mother said, scowling at Tony.

He looked into her eyes for a moment – those eyes that had once been beautiful and as blue as the sea, but now looked as if all the life had been drained from them. There was nothing to be seen in them but emptiness and hopelessness. He also remembered seeing them brimming with hatred and anger. When she snarled like this, he could see her brown teeth.

'Don't dance now, Tony,' she said clearly, and he came to his senses.

'Of course I'll dance, Mum. You've always wanted me to dance for you. We're not going to break that habit now,' he said, stripping off his clothes.

He sat on the floor to put on ballet shoes.

'You don't need ballet shoes. Boys don't dance in those,' she said, breaking into tears.

'What do you mean, Mum? You always had me dance in ballet shoes. Don't you remember?' he said, opening the sideboard and taking out two elastic bands 'You wanted me to grow and for my insteps to be broader. Of course I dance in ballet shoes,' he continued, pulling his hair back and snapping the bands around it. He effortlessly placed the bun low against the back of his neck.

'Hey, let's have a drink,' he said, holding her head as he poured vodka into her mouth until she began to retch. 'Look,' he said, stepping quickly over to the sideboard and picking up a yellowing, dog-eared script that lay on it. 'See? Here it is. This is what we need to rehearse, Mum. You know your choreography has to be just right. What shall we go for now?' he continued, flicking through the script. 'The wolf? Nooo. We've already mastered that one. What about the dragon? Let's try that one. I need to get this one right.'

'Stop it now. I don't want this. I don't want you to dance any more. I can't...'

She fell silent as Tony went to the record player and dropped the needle onto a record. Bach's loud, delicate tones emanated from paired loudspeakers at each corner of the room.

Tony stood naked before her. He closed his eyes, lifted his arms high in a smooth movement, and his upper body swayed back. He lifted himself onto his toes, bent to one side until gravity took over, and floated with silent steps over the living room floor.

5

'Valdi, my love. Valdi. You have to sit up. There's a phone call for you,' his wife said as she stooped over Valdimar who was stretched out on the sofa, taking a post-Friday-night-dinner nap.

He opened his eyes, and it took him a moment to take everything in. These naps of his were becoming deeper and heavier as he grew older, and these days he simply needed a little more time when he awoke to work out if he was still in dreamland. He blinked rapidly and stared at his wife.

'Yes, my dear. You're awake. There's someone on the phone for you,' she said, gesturing to the phone in its alcove that led off from the living room.

He sighed heavily, levered himself up with reluctance and went over to the phone. He blamed the sofa's worn-out springs for how much of a struggle it was to get up from it. His wife was more inclined to blame it on his weight gain, and he knew perfectly well that she was right. He picked up the grey receiver and spoke his name. He listened for a long time. He finished the call with the words, 'I'm coming.'

'What now?' Ásta asked, without looking up as he came into the kitchen. He had sniffed out the aroma of coffee long before he stood at her side by the kitchen worktop, where she poured boiling water through the coffee filter. There was nothing unusual about these calls, considering he had been a police officer for close to fifty years and was now approaching retirement. They had first got to know each other when he had been a brand-new twenty-year-old police recruit, immensely proud of standing on the traffic island wearing white gloves that reached his elbows, holding a wooden truncheon of the same colour as he directed the traffic. He had joined CID when it was established in 1977.

'They've found him.'

'Found who?'

'The American. The one who was thought to have lost his life in that aircraft on Hofsjökull,' he said, running his fingers through his longish grey hair.

'And they found him up there on the ice cap?' Ásta asked, pouring coffee for him as he stood expectant with a cup in his hand.

'No. Not at all. They found him right here in Reykjavík.'

6

Valdimar arrived at the pathology building on Barónsstígur and went along the badly lit corridor. At the far end, he saw his longstanding colleague Ævar, one of the country's most experienced forensic pathologists. It seemed to Valdimar that although they had known each other for a long time, Ævar hadn't changed at all. He stood ramrod-straight, in his white lab coat and with tousled white hair, and – of course – with far too many pens in his breast pocket. Next to him stood a young woman, and Valdimar was sure he hadn't seen her before.

'Hello, Valdimar. My name's Ylfa', she said as he approached, extending a hand. She looked him up and down, but that wasn't enough for her to catch his eye. She was far too petite, and he was much too tall for her to look him in the eye.

Valdimar sized up this young, small, mousy-haired woman, who could hardly have been more than twenty-six or twenty-seven, now watching him with determined green eyes. The green faded a little as she unwound a thick, dark green scarf from around her neck. He noticed a delicate nose with a red tip as she sniffed. Valdimar offered her a handkerchief, which Ylfa waved away.

'Good evening,' he said, guessing that she had just arrived, as her hand was cold. 'I'm sure I've seen you before,' he said, hesitatingly.

'You think so? Could be,' she said, sounding a little

insecure. 'I haven't been with CID long and haven't had to deal with many murder cases. No so far, at any rate. But you might have seen me in the canteen,' she added with a smile.

'Anyway, you've been given this case,' Valdimar said amiably.

'Yes', she laughed. 'That's maybe because I was with the investigation team at the air crash site on Hofsjökull,' she said, sniffing again.

'Here,' Valdimar said, again offering the handkerchief. 'It's clean and you can keep it.'

He had been to Germany several times over the years on CID business, where more than once it had been pointed out to him that sniffing audibly was considered the height of vulgarity.

Ævar had been shuffling his feet next to them and seemed relieved that their exchange was over. He took them into the cool lab, having first asked them to remove their shoes. The place was tiled in white from floor to ceiling, and the floor was icy. In spite of the overwhelming smell of surgical alcohol and disinfectant, Valdimar sensed the distinctive stench that he knew was nothing other than the smell of death. He saw the body, laid out on a steel table in the centre of the room. It had sometimes occurred to him that it would be simply and completely wrong if someone were to make an effort to turn the morgue into a more welcoming place.

He looked around and saw that he had been mistaken. Some brave soul had placed an illuminated Father Christmas on top of the coffee machine.

The windows high in the walls of the room were wide open and ice-cold air flooded in. Without asking permission, Valdimar reached for the pole hook and pulled a window shut. He hadn't imagined that he might be taking a liberty, but Ævar stood still, hands in the pockets of his lab coat, and glared in disapproval. Valdimar decided to leave it at that. They had known each other a long time.

'It's not without good reason that this place needs to be cold...'

'Ævar, you're wearing slippers. My socks are literally freezing to the floor,' he interrupted and noticed Ylfa look up and smile.

Ævar didn't reply, but Valdimar was sure there was a smirk on his face.

'What can you tell us?' Valdimar asked.

'Well, he's been dead for a good long time,' Ævar began, standing at the head of the table. 'I'd say at least six months.'

Valdimar and Ylfa stood side by side and looked down at the human remains in poor condition in front of them. There had already been a great deal of decomposition and the face was hardly recognisable as human. An oval steel dish stood on a corner of the table at the foot end. On it lay a foot.

'And you're sure it's this John?' Valdimar asked.

'We found identification on him,' Ylfa said.

Valdimar took the plastic sleeve containing the documents. 'John Michael Antonelli,' he muttered to himself. 'Was he Italian?'

'Yes, or of Italian descent.'

'And how did he turn up?'

'Some kids playing in the old army barracks on the western side of Öskjuhlíð, just below the tanks. They were messing about with a pile of stones in there when they saw a shoe. They gave it a pull, and that came out with it,' she said, indicating the foot in its steel dish.

'How come it hadn't been found before? There are kids playing up there all the time,' Valdimar said.

'It had been bundled up in a tarpaulin and was hard up against the wall, with stones piled over it. And you're right. The kids who found him often play there. I spoke to one of the boys and he said that there had been a bad smell in there back in the summer. They thought it must have been a dead cat or a rat.' 'And what do you think happened here?'

'It's not easy to tell,' said Ævar, who stood at the dead man's hip. 'The body is badly decomposed, and I still have to do a more thorough examination. But,' he said, with a new emphasis, 'the skull is fractured at the back of the head, and he was murdered, as there's an incision with a sharp instrument to the abdomen and two in the region of the heart,' he said, pointing them out.

Ylfa and Valdimar leaned closer and between the folds of brown skin the indistinct incisions could be made out.

'This was a pretty big knife,' Valdimar said.

'Yes, we can go on that assumption. It is of course uncertain how far the weapon penetrated, but the largest wound is about four point three centimetres across,' Ævar said, looking up from the report in his hands. 'There's something else about this that's interesting,' he said, going over to a table by the wall.

Valdimar and Ylfa followed and stood in front of a rolled-up tarpaulin that had been placed on a metal iron tray.

'The body was trussed up in this tarpaulin, which was presumably originally white. I don't know if it's relevant, but the smell attracted my interest,' he said.

'What sort of smell?' Ylfa asked.

'Look at these stains,' he said, lifting the tarpaulin onto another table and partially unrolling it. 'These stains that are almost black are blood. But these lighter marks are something else,' he continued, leaning close to one and sniffing. 'It's barely perceptible, but there's a smell of varnish to this.'

Valdimar and Ylfa followed his lead and sniffed the tarpaulin. 'Is that some kind of oil?' Valdimar asked. 'It's wood varnish,' Ylfa said, sounding certain. 'We've been varnishing an old dining table at home and it's exactly the same smell,' she said, sniffing it again.

'I've sent a sample for further analysis and hopefully

we'll get some results before long,' Ævar said, rolling up the tarpaulin again.

7

'You said you were involved in the investigation when he disappeared?' Valdimar asked when he and Ylfa had emerged into the bitter cold outside, both of them relieved to be back in the fresh air.

'Yes. That was the first case I worked on. There was nothing to indicate that he hadn't lost his life up there on the ice cap,' she said, the chagrin plain in her voice. 'It's come like a bolt from the blue to find him dead, and especially here on Öskjuhlíð.'

'I remember that case. There was someone with him, wasn't there?' he said, buttoning his woollen coat and adjusting his scarf as they crossed the road to the car park.

'Yep. John was a pilot, but was no longer able to fly. There had been some problem with his eyesight. So he took a friend with him who had a pilot's licence. John had been an Air Force officer and had been on the base here from 1960 to 1963. He was here with his family, that's his wife and three children,' she said, fishing from the pocket of her sheepskin coat a pair of gloves that looked to have been knitted from the same wool as her scarf. 'I've faxed the Directorate of Immigration for more information about his presence in Iceland, but right now we don't have any record of him coming back to Iceland until around six months ago. That was when he arrived here with this friend of his and they were going to fetch an aircraft and deliver it to the US. Before leaving they intended to go to Akureyri to pick up some spare parts. There was a thick fog over the highlands, and they crash-landed on Hofsjökull. The wreckage was scattered over a wide area, and the search teams only found John's companion. It was an incredibly difficult search as the terrain is challenging, with fissures everywhere. They didn't find any sign of John.'

'And it was confirmed that he was in the aircraft?' he asked, standing next to the 1970 model Saab 96 which some had speculated was nothing more than a Volkswagen Beetle that had been stretched and flattened.

'Yes, or so we thought,' she said, admiring the car. 'We spoke to plenty of people. Witnesses, the air traffic authority and others. They all said that he had gone with him.'

'What did John do? Was he still in the military?'

'No. He'd made a lot of money and he bought and sold aircraft and spare parts. It seems he had bought this aircraft they had come to fetch. And he has quite a lot of property here.'

'What sort of property?'

'Well. I need to go back through the case notes. If I recall correctly, there's some land in the east, office space, and a detached house here in Reykjavík.'

'So,' Valdimar said, glancing at his watch to see that it was almost ten. 'We can go over it all in the morning,' he said and opened the car door. 'Was this property checked out?'

'What do you mean?'

'Well, whether there's anyone here in Iceland who has access to it or manages it, that kind of thing.'

'No, I don't think so,' she said slowly. 'Checking that wasn't really part of our remit. We saw no reason to, considering it was believed that he had lost his life in the crash. That was the end of our involvement with the case,' she said, and Valdimar could make out from her tone of voice that she was seeking to justify herself.

'All right. Do you need a lift?' 'No. My car's here.'

'Fine. We'll look into it tomorrow. Good night,' he said, getting into the car. He turned the key, but it was stubborn, and the engine only burst noisily into life on the fourth attempt. He pretended not to see Ylfa, who had turned away. Glancing in the mirror as he drove away, he was sure there was a smile on her face, and he decided that it might be time to take a look at the exhaust.

THE DANCER

8

Tony swore to himself as he walked into the National Theatre as it was approaching nine o'clock. He had meant to be there before eight, but he had been delayed, absorbed in the dance.

When he finally realised how late it was, he had switched off the music and helped his mother into bed. He was about to leave her room when his mother asked where he was going. He went over to her and put his face close to hers.

'A dance practice, mum. I'm going to a rehearsal at the National Theatre.'

A scowl appeared on her face. On his way out he heard her mutter something about him not being allowed to go to dance class.

Tony opened the doors cautiously and was relieved to see that the stage was empty. There was silence in the deserted auditorium, and an unearthly golden light whispered its way through the vault, styled to resemble columns of basalt high above his head. He went slowly up the steps as if unwilling to break the silence, then squeezed along a row of seats in the middle of the auditorium as he ran a hand over the red felt covering of the chair backs. Tony looked down at the spray of leaves and the two faces embroidered on every single one. One face appeared petrified; the other livid. He looked at the boxes on each side of the stage and decided that these had to be intended for better-heeled members of the audience.

He had never before set foot inside this place that his grandfather had told him used to be referred to as an Elves' palace, when he had invited Tony to see a show with him many years before. He must have been ten or eleven? He didn't remember. But he remembered when his mother refused to allow him to go. The reasons were lost in the mists of the past. There were all kinds of things she wouldn't allow. Yes, and he recalled that his grandfather had also told him when he was around twenty that he had worked on the building when the British had requisitioned the place during the war as a munitions store.

The silence was broken as some dancers appeared, making their way onto the stage, and Tony sat deeper in his seat. He could feel the tension rise inside him. He wasn't sure whether or not to cross his legs. He didn't. He clasped his knee as it began to pump rapidly up and down.

'Hæ,' he heard someone call out. He looked up at the stage and saw Hulda smile and wave to him. He shyly waved back.

'Hulda, take your position,' instructed a bony woman who marched with quick steps onto the stage and stood there, ramrod straight. 'I can't be doing with any messing about today. We have too much ground to cover.'

We have too much ground to cover, Tony thought. *We have too much ground to cover.* The words echoed in his head. No, they didn't so much echo as bounce off the inside of his skull, as if someone had hurled the words at his brain, and he put his hands to his head. He stared at the dancers on the stage that seemed to dissolve through a haze to become his mother's living room. He saw the glassless painting, the embroidered pictures, the living room clock that had long ago stopped chiming the hours. That was missing its glass front, shattered when his mother had missed her target when she had hurled a potted plant meant for... He didn't remember the guy's name. He was just another of those unknown faces who visited his mother, either to get inside her or to cadge a drink. He also saw the worn chair with its threadbare cover, burn marks and the little tears in the upholstery through which the white padding squeezed itself out. And there was his mother, who sat in this revolting chair with a glass of vodka in her hand and a scowl on her face as the cigarette smoke curled upwards into her eyes.

While he stood in the middle of the floor.

Tony watched his mother take out the record. She looked for a long time at the picture on the sleeve and he struggled to make out whether there was a shadow of a smile or a grimace that formed on her lips. He was far from sure. It was getting more difficult to figure out her expressions. It was so unpredictable, as she could react in completely the opposite way to what could be expected from the look on her face. But most likely, this was a scowl after all, because the smoke from the cigarette in the corner of her mouth was getting in her eyes.

She extracted the record from the sleeve and placed it with the utmost caution on the record player, as carefully as when she lifted a brimming wineglass to her lips. She took the cigarette from her mouth as she leaned forward in the armchair to lift the player's arm, peer at it and blow on the needle.

'Mum, can I...?'

'Shhh,' *she said, dropping the needle onto the record's outermost edge. Delicate clicks carried from the veneered speakers in each corner of the room.*

'Mum, can't I have my birthday present now?' *he said, his eyes on the little packet tied in ribbon with a bow on the table at her side, and he ran a hand over the bald patch on the top of his head, the result of his mother in a fit of anger cropping his hair too close with an electric shaver.*

'Not until you can do this perfectly,' *she said absently, leaning back in the chair, puffing her cigarette and blowing the smoke from the opposite corner of her mouth. That was accompanied by a gulp of Bacardi mixed with a little water.*

'We've already been through this, Tony. You get it right, you get the present. Otherwise, you don't. You're nine years old and the sooner you realise that you don't get a present without doing something for it, the better. I've told you a thousand times. There are two different worlds, as I've told you. There's a hard world and there's a bad world. And we live in both of them. That's the world with no perks or gifts. I know all about that,' she said, half-closing her eyes.

The sweet strains of Bach emerged from the speakers. To begin with the melody was carried by the beautiful, delicate tones of violins and cellos, with other instruments joining in as the piece progressed. The music gained in volume and the kettle drums thundered faster, deeper. Then there was a sudden silence.

'Ready to dance, my boy,' his mother said, her voice gentle. The strings began to resonate after the silence.

Tony stood still and stared down at the floor. He looked down at his feet, bound from instep to ankle. He picked out both old and new bloodstains on the bindings, left by the ballet shoes his mother made him dance in every day. He didn't react when he saw the blood that was right now seeping to the surface. The scab had been torn off as his mother had bound his feet earlier. It never got to heal properly. It had bled as well when she had made him dance that morning. It was as if the bloodstain was a living, red animal in its own right, flourishing there on his instep, spreading through the finely woven material.

'Mum, my feet really hurt. I don't want to dance. And everyone's making fun of me. The boys asked the other day if they could see... see my pussy. Can't we stop now? And I really want my present.'

'Hell!' She snapped upright with a peculiarly sharp movement, as if her body hadn't been ready but had all the same done its best to follow orders from her brain. She pulled the needle off the record without first lifting it clear of the surface and the loudspeakers wailed in protest. Cigarette ash fell to the floor.

'Look! Look what you made me do, you wretched boy. I...

sorry, I didn't mean to... Let's try again. You know as well as anyone that you're supposed to start after the first pause,' she said, the softness in her voice in contrast to the anger that shone from her face.

Tony quailed, and instantly felt the urge to pee. In the past, under these circumstances, the pee had flooded out without warning, but he had learned to fool the messages his nerves sent, keeping it back.

She placed the needle back on the record and the music again came to life. The kettle drums thundered and then came the pause.

Tony stood still.

'Dance, boy!' his mother screeched.

Tony jerked into movement, hands above his head in a graceful arch. He raised his left leg so the sole touched his right knee. His hips swung in smooth circles, and he lifted himself onto his toes. He crouched, and his right foot effortlessly propelled him upright as his left unfolded like a leaf. His limbs swayed and twisted, with sensitive, precise movements, as he twirled, leaped or lay on the floor. He shimmered silently like a silk scarf. The tragic notes faded and came to an end with the single fading note of a violin.

Tony lay in a heap on the floor for a moment after the music had come to an end, before getting to his feet. He looked at his mother as the tears rolled down his cheeks.

'Can I have my present now, mum?'

Her mind appeared to be somewhere far away, but the question brought her back to her senses. She upended the contents of the glass down her throat and stood up.

'No. We have too much ground to cover. In fact, much more than just much... There's no present now,' she said, and went into the kitchen.

She returned, made herself comfortable in the chair and placed the needle at the beginning of the record.

'Dance,' she said, almost sadly. Tony stood still and stared at her with blank eyes. 'Tony!' she howled.

9

'Tony? Tony?'

Startled, he looked up and to the side, to see the dance instructor seated next to him. He wasn't sure if it was the fact that she had spoken his name, or the penetrating smell of nutmeg about her that had taken him unawares.

'Your name's Tony, isn't it?' she asked in a German accent, unsmiling. He looked back at her plump, strong face. He wondered if she had facial muscles capable of generating a smile.

'Yes,' he said, almost cautiously.

'They told me you can dance,' she said, jerking her head in the direction of the stage where the dancers were taking a break, sitting on the floor. 'Have you trained in ballet?'

'Yes,' he said quietly, feeling immediately insecure as he nodded his head.

The teacher looked into his eyes for a long time, as if she could read something from his face. Too much reading, he thought.

'My name is Birgitte. They call me Begga. I know they call me the Witch when they think I don't hear them,' she said, winking. 'Would you like to practise with us? We are always short of male dancers.'

Yes, there's a shadow there, he thought. Just the shadow of a smile.

'I don't know. I...'

'Excellent!' she said, getting to her feet. 'Do you have a

training kit with you?'

'No.'

'Oddur,' she called up to the stage. 'Would you go with Tony and find him something to train in?'

'Good to see you. So you decided to join us?' Oddur said as he climbed the stairs at a run, going to the upper floor where the dance school had its practice room. They went through the long room and to the dressing room.

'Have you been dancing long?' Oddur asked. He was bare-chested and pushed a lock of red hair back from his face. He rooted through a cardboard box marked unclaimed items. 'What size are you?'

'What clothes are you looking for?'

Oddur stared in surprise.

'Just trackie bottoms or something. You aren't going to dance in your underwear, are you? Unless you want to,' he laughed. 'Where are you from, anyway?'

'Meaning what?' Tony asked, although he was fully aware of the reason for the question.

For as long as he could remember, he had heard disparaging comments. His southern looks had attracted mercilessly negative attention. His schoolmates had branded him one of the ten little niggers, even though his skin was only marginally darker than theirs. It was a favourite to call him the Sambo Kid, and many of them had asked if his mother had been a US army whore. The older generation had used the word mulatto, which he had at first failed to understand.

His mother had refused to explain that time she had knocked a woman flat in the grocery store.

'Well, you know...'

'Iceland. I'm from here. From Reykjavík,' he said and glared at Oddur, who looked away as he glowered, and went back to rooting through the box.

Tony noticed scratches on Oddur's back that looked fresh.

He was slim, but powerfully built. His muscles bunched visibly beneath his pale white skin.

'Here. These should fit,' he said at last, tossing a pair of trousers to him. Tony flinched, concerned that Oddur had noticed him checking out his physique.

Tony looked at the track suit bottoms, which looked to be ripped at the knees.

'Just put them on, man. We don't have all day. The Witch is waiting.'

Tony pulled off his jeans and noticed from the corner of his eye Oddur eyeing him.

'What? You're not shy, are you?' Oddur asked, running his fingers through his thick hair as Tony glanced at him.

They went to the stage, where Begga was haranguing a technician who was telling her that the electrics weren't working properly, and they would have to make do with limited lighting, but it would all be in order before too long.

Begga came over to them, took Tony by the hand and led him to the edge of the stage.

'We're rehearsing a routine that will be shown in a week or so as part of the City of Reykjavík's Christmas festival of culture. Your part is actually not complicated, so you should pick it up quickly. That's assuming you really can dance,' she said with a smile, and without looking at him. 'If you go over to the girls there and follow them, I'll instruct you,' she said, switching on the music.

Tony could feel the insecurity well up inside him as he took a few steps across the stage. He could feel the eyes of these twenty-six dancers on him. He looked up to meet Hulda's encouraging gaze as she stood on the tips of her toes, arms lifted high. Her fair hair was tied in a stiff bun at the back of her head and her slim, statuesque figure was reminiscent of a feather.

Tony took his place by the group of girls and noticed Oddur smiling warmly in his direction. A little too warmly, he felt. Begga's powerful voice echoed over the stage as she criticised, provided advice and instructions on positioning and everything else in French. Tony did his best to follow the girls' movements but missed his footing a little on one of the steps.

'Stop, stop,' Begga called out, pausing the music. 'Are you wearing socks?' she asked in disdain, then looked in Tony's direction.

He didn't reply but felt the pressure increasing in his head as he sensed that every eye was on him. He longed to run from the stage.

'All right. Take them off and we'll go again,' Begga ordered, clapping her hands twice.

The music again boomed out.

Tony followed the girls' lead, but as had happened while he sat in the auditorium, the vision of the dancers began to blur until they vanished into the haze. He was alone on the stage, running the length of it and spinning in circles. He felt himself glide through the heavy air. He lifted onto his toes as if he were wearing ballet shoes, stepped and spun countless times. The music slowed and enveloped him, as soft as honey, as he swayed like a tall, lonely reed.

It was as if he had been torn up by the roots when he heard the calls.

'Stop, stop, stop!' Begga cried out, clapping her hands three times. The music stopped. 'What on earth is going on?' she rasped, hardly able to speak through her astonishment as she stood with her shoulders slumped, as if she had been punctured. 'What was that?' she continued, making her way directly to Tony. It wasn't easy to work out whether her tone of voice was shock or adulation.

Tony stood stock still and felt his heart race. He stared down at Begga where she had halted in front of him. She opened her mouth and was about to say something when the lights that had malfunctioned earlier came to life, bathing the stage in light. Begga took a sharp breath, and her hands went to her mouth as she saw his feet.

Tony looked down at his gnarled feet, as did everyone on the stage. He looked up, had an urge to brush away the tears he felt were running down his cheeks. But he wasn't so sure. Maybe it was some other emotion at work. Perhaps it was the fury and the intensity that rushed to the surface, forcing its way out of every opening in his head, which seemed about to burst. He looked around him and saw the indistinct outlines of the dancers lined up in front of him.

He ran from the stage and fled.

10

Saturday, 4th December 1982

'Who finished the biscuits?' Valdimar asked, as he walked into the canteen on the second floor of the main police station on Hverfisgata. He held the empty packet and his eyes picked out each of the five officers around the table. Three of them were clear suspects, cheeks puffed like hamsters and the scattering of biscuit crumbs in front of each of them gave them away. 'I hope they don't choke you.'

'Are there any more biscuits?' one of them asked, after taking a gulp of coffee to help him swallow.

There was some stifled laughter, but Valdimar didn't look their way.

'Anyone for sand cake?' said Ylfa as she came in. 'Baked it last night,' she said happily, placing the circular cake on the table.

'Isn't it on the small side?' one of the officers asked, inspecting the cake that fitted neatly onto a saucer.

'It's not small. It's just... modestly sized,' she replied, sounding offended.

They went to Valdimar's office and Ylfa put the saucer and the cake on his desk. He took a seat in his fabric-covered chair and looked at the desk in front of him. He adjusted the papers and the photograph in a gold-coloured frame showing his grandchildren and another of himself in full uniform and a white helmet astride a Harley-Davidson motorcycle.

'Did you find the case notes?' he asked Ylfa, who had sat down in the chair facing the desk.

'Yes, it should all be here,' she said, opening a folder she had placed on the desk alongside a cardboard box containing those of John's worldly possessions that had been on him when his body had been found. 'And here's a list of his assets in Iceland,' she continued, handing it to Valdimar.

He took the list, which covered three sheets of paper.

Ylfa watched Valdimar as he scanned the list, and quickly looked down at the folder in her lap when she sensed he had noticed her gaze. She didn't know what it was – some kind of trepidation, blended with respect. Since joining the department, she had heard a great deal about Valdimar. In fact, it went back a lot further than that as he was often spoken of as if he were a legend with practically rock star status. Her vision of him hadn't gone quite that far, although she couldn't escape the pleasant but unreal feeling of satisfaction that she was working with him on this case.

'I've sent a fax requesting information on who manages these properties and deals with his tax affairs,' she said and cut herself a slice of cake. 'Aren't you going to have any?'

'What? No, no thanks. My doctor would have a fit,' he said without looking up from the documents in front of him. 'He has this two-hundred-and-fifty-hectare piece of land in Mjóafjörður, as well as commercial premises on Ármúli that's no less than two thousand, three hundred square metres. I think it's where the tanning place is,' he said, taking off his glasses and catching Ylfa's eye.

'Tanning place?'

'Yes, the place where we nabbed a burglar who went in there to use the sun beds. He was pretty tired of the winter darkness,' he said, smiling and readjusting his glasses.

'There's a bunch of companies in that building, so there must be a decent rental income from it. So where does the money go?'

'And there's the detached house on the list as well,' Ylfa said through a mouthful of cake.

'What was that?'

She parked the piece of cake in one cheek.

'I said, there's also that detached house on the list.'

'That's right. On Öldugata, which he bought in 1963. He acquired the land in the east in 1970, the commercial premises eight years later, so he must have been back and forth here after he left the Air Force. When was that?'

She skimmed a couple of pages in the folder.

'August that same year. That's 1963.'

'Exactly. He buys a house and then leaves the country shortly afterwards,' Valdimar said thoughtfully. 'Do we know...' he began, but was interrupted by a knock on the door and a police officer's cheerful face appeared in the doorway.

'Excuse me. Here's the fax you were waiting for, Ylfa,' he said, handed her a sheet of paper and was gone.

'A lawyer in Garðabær has looked after John's affairs. Baldur...'

'Baldur Viðars?' Valdimar broke in, snatching his glasses from his face.

'Yes,' she said in surprise. 'You know him?'

'Yes. We're members of the same order.'

'Order?' Ylfa asked, failing to understand.

'The Order of Freemasons,' he said after a pause, and focused again on the property list.

'Are you in the Freemasons?' she asked, immediately regretting the edge of derision in her voice. Her brother had joined the order and she had made unstinting fun of him, not of the order itself, but of him when she had seen him dressed in the regalia, the stiff formal dress and the stovepipe hat.

'Yes,' he said.

'And?'

'And what?'

'Then shouldn't we pay Baldur the Freemason a visit?'

'Yep,' he said and stood up. 'Let's drop in and see him,' he continued, picking up a slice of cake on the way out.

11

Tony looked out of the kitchen window. He thought he had heard a racket outside the door. It was just nine o'clock and it was still dark outside. Grettisgata's street lights were barely able to throw their brightness as far as the backs of the houses. The constant snow blown off nearby roofs didn't help. There was nothing unusual about this noise. Far too many people saw the tall grey aspen in front of the dark entrance leading to the back flat as a perfect place to pee.

Tony rented the back flat, which was in reality more of a shed, from the elderly lady who lived in the house that faced the street. It had been her bright idea to get Tony to crown the tree with a string of Christmas lights. The display of lights, which also flickered, certainly discouraged people, but had the disadvantage of keeping her awake, as the crown of the tree was level with her bedroom window on the upper floor. Finally, she unplugged it, so the tree's Christmas spirit was short-lived.

Standing at the kitchen window, lost in thought, Tony was hauled back to reality as he felt water around his feet. He hurried to the little bathroom and turned off the tap. He had completely forgotten that he had used the shower hose to fill a tub. He swore as he saw the water that had flooded the floor and into the kitchen. He had been meaning to ask the old lady about getting the drain in the shower unblocked, getting a shower head for the hose, fixing the cracked window in the living room, as well as a few other repairs that needed to be done about the place that came to mind. He had continued to mention all these repairs to the landlady ever since he had moved in six months ago. *It'll be done in a day or two*, she always blithely replied. And it was still *in a day or two*. When he had mopped the floor dry, he took the tub to the kitchenette and put it on the floor in front of the kitchen chair. He gingerly immersed his feet in the hot water, picked up a little flask from the kitchen table and peered at the thick, yellow contents.

The day before, Tony had got lost in the passages of the National Theatre when he fled from the stage. Going down one dead end after another left him so confused that he had no idea where in the building he was. He had felt that he was shut in and was about to open a window in the dark corridor simply to get his breath. Unable to open the window's fastenings, he crouched down. He had the feeling that his heart was pounding so hard that it was about to burst loose, and he was practically unable to stop himself hyperventilating.

'Tony,' a female voice along the passage called out.

'What do you want?' he asked when he saw Hulda coming towards him.

'I... Nothing. I just saw you ran the wrong way when you left the auditorium. It's so easy to get lost here if you don't know your way around. I was scared shitless the first time I got lost in here. They'd all convinced me that the place is infested with theatre ghosts,' she said, laughing. 'Aren't your clothes upstairs?'

'Yes,' he said, staring out of the window, focusing his mind on regaining control of his breathing.

'Come with me,' she murmured, placing a cautious hand on his shoulder. 'The training room is at the far end of the building.'

Tony was sure that she smiled, even though he couldn't see it.

She took him up to fetch his clothes, and then to the theatre's main entrance.

'Here. Try this on your feet. It'll soften and heal them,' she said, handing him a flask. 'My grandmother makes it.' Tony took the flask and looked into her eyes.

'Don't you dance in ballet shoes, Tony?' she asked, with concern in her voice.

'Thanks,' he replied quickly, turned and went down the steps. 'There's a practice at the same time tomorrow night,' she called out as he reached the pavement. 'It would be great to see you again.'

He unscrewed the cap of the flask, and the thick oil formed a film on the hot water. It snaked like a jellyfish, curling beneath the surface, closer and closer to his blackened, bruised, twisted feet.

12

They walked into the rather cramped offices of Baldur's legal practice on Borgartún. Baldur courteously introduced himself to Ylfa after hugging Valdimar as they patted each other's shoulders and quickly dispensed with the formalities.

'Sorry to disturb you during the weekend. And thanks for being able to meet at such short notice,' Valdimar said.

'Ach, don't worry about it. I'm here day in and day out, and gave up on weekends long ago. I was about to go and call in on Öldugata. Nobody there answers the phone or replies to the letters I've been sending.'

'So who's living there?' Valdimar asked when they had made themselves comfortable in chairs facing the wide desk, holding cups of coffee that Baldur brought them. Each caught the other's eye with a questioning look just as they both were about to place a cup on the only patch of clear space to be seen anywhere on the desk that was piled high with stacks of papers. Some of these had turned yellow and looked to have been untouched for years. There was so much else that hadn't been moved, Valdimar thought as he glanced around. Around two years had passed since he had last called on Baldur. The Mont Blanc pen set was in its place on the window sill, on top of the legal almanac listing the country's legal profession, next to a 1979 Hampiðjan calendar. There were a couple of valuable original paintings on the walls, and a Muggur watercolour hung on the wall behind Baldur, slightly crooked.

Baldur pulled a sheaf of papers from one of the stacks and leafed unerringly through it, licking the tip of a bone-dry index finger, worn thin by years of handling paperwork.

'Gunnhildur Jónsdóttir. She's lived there with her son since 1963 when John bought the house,' he said, reaching forward to hand the document to Valdimar.

'She's been renting the house all that time?'

'Not at all. She's never paid a penny in rent,' he said, leaning forward and looking at them over the top of his reading glasses. 'He bought this property and subsequently handed it over to Gunnhildur so that she paid no rent and no costs. John dealt with everything. That means property tax, electricity, heating, the whole lot, for how long...? Nineteen years. I handled these payments on his behalf, as I have dealt with other properties of his here.'

'Why on earth did he do that?' Ylfa asked.

'That's a good question,' Baldur said, twisting a green biro with a Búnaðarbanki logo in his fingers. 'I never got to the bottom of it. I tried, discreetly, to ask about all this, back then,' he said, polishing the lenses of his glasses with the end of his purple tie, and holding them up to the light. 'But he never gave me an answer.'

'There must be a connection there,' said Ylfa, taking the document from Valdimar. 'Have you met this woman?'

'No. Never.' The glasses were back in place, perched on his nose. 'I've never had reason to. Well, until now. And she's not replying.'

'What's your reason now for getting in touch with her?' Valdimar asked.

'Because of property tax and suchlike. John was married and the family in Fort Lauderdale want to see these properties sold. They knew about the land and the commercial premises, but they had no idea about the house on Öldugata. They had even less idea that he had been paying all the costs associated with the property all these years. I don't know how they found this out, but their lawyer contacted me to ask about it. All I could tell him was that I handle the relevant payments. I suppose they must have found some old paperwork.'

'So the family over there is presumably going to sell the place from under Gunnhildur?' Valdimar said.

'No,' Baldur said, glancing at them in turn.

'And?'

'All right,' he said, hesitating, and getting to his feet. He sighed, turned to the window, and gazed at the view of Mount Esja and its snow-covered slopes. 'Maybe I've been economical with the truth. I got to know John in 1963 when he bought the house on Öldugata. I wasn't a close friend of his, but we respected each other, and our dealings have always been completely painless. He took care to make it plain that there were certain things I wasn't to mention to anyone. Of course, as a lawyer, I took this very seriously and have always honoured his wishes. John was always punctilious, and he was an honest man. On the other hand, he met Gunnhildur when he was working at the base, got her pregnant and she had a boy. I know nothing of how this all took place,' he said, and paused. 'Forbidden fruits, I imagine,' he continued and smiled briefly. 'I met his family on three occasions when I had reason to call on him at the base. I had no inkling that this was anything other than a happy marriage. But he confided in me concerning Gunnhildur and he was deeply distressed about the whole thing. She had come after him and threatened to tell his wife if he didn't buy her a house and pay her maintenance,' he said, and sat down again. 'It didn't help that he was of Italian heritage, and they have their own ways of doing things. He felt himself honour-bound to go along with her wishes. But I know he was also sympathetic to Gunnhildur,' he said with emphasis. 'She hasn't... She probably never had an easy time of it. I understand that she had encountered a number of misfortunes and drank rather heavily. He said that she was unpredictable and could have blown his family and even the whole extended family apart. He bought this house, and that's where I came in. I assisted with the whole thing. But he also signed an agreement with her.'

'What sort of agreement?' Ylfa asked.

'The house was registered in his name. But under the terms of the agreement, she is the real owner of the property.'

'Why did he want to do it like that?' Valdimar asked, sipping coffee which was cold by now.

'Primarily because she wanted it that way. I don't think she trusted herself. She had been in all kinds of trouble and wanted the house to be secure from creditors if she were to do something stupid. There was less chance of that happening if he was the registered owner, so she didn't want to run any risk of losing the house. The whole process was an absolute nightmare because she had ... excuse my French ... an arsehole of a lawyer looking after her side of it and the outcome was that the right of inheritance goes her way. So her son is the legal inheritor of the house,' he said, opening a locked cabinet by his side. He leafed through documents and handed Valdimar the agreement. 'I don't know if this is of any relevance to you ... and I know I'm breaking my word. But I thought it right to tell you.'

13

'Tony,' his mother called from the bedroom. 'What are you up to?'

'Just cleaning up,' he said as he went into her room, pulling off his drab rubber gloves and putting the scrubbing brush down on the bedside table. Tony lifted his mother's head and straightened the pillow, picked up the glass that stood on the table and helped her gulp tepid water.

She swallowed with difficulty.

'Have you been here long?'

'No. Not long.'

'What's the time, anyway?'

'It's about twelve, midday,' he replied, when he had glanced from force of habit at the alarm clock that stood on the bedside table, and which had long ceased to tell the time. It must be around twelve, he thought. He had noticed the Persil clock on Lækjartorg as it had struck ten. After bathing his feet he had left the house, when the landlady had called out from the window, asking if he would be such a darling as to shovel the snow from her steps. That had taken him an hour and then he had gone to Vísir to buy bread, milk and salami. Shopping hadn't been at the top of his list of priorities. He had hoped to run into the dancers, but they were nowhere to be seen.

'Why do you always clean the kitchen?' she asked, looking hard at him. 'You're always scrubbing it. Can't you clean something else? The living room, or my bedroom?'

'Everything's fine in here, Mum,' he said absent-mindedly.

'No, it most certainly isn't,' she said, running a trembling finger over the edge of the bedside table and showing him the thick smear of grease and dust on her fingertip. 'That's not clean.'

'It's cleaner than my room has been my entire life, Mum. You've nothing to complain about,' he said steadily. 'Aren't you hungry?' he added hurriedly, as she seemed about to protest.

'Yes,' she said, and seemed to have immediately forgotten what they had been squabbling over. 'You're not going to give me that meat stew again for lunch?'

'No. I'll make us some sandwiches,' he said and switched on the radio that occupied the open drawer of the bedside table, and the state radio station's jingle echoed from it.

Tony was about to leave when the newsreader's familiar voice began to list the main news items.

According to a police statement, the body of a man was found in the abandoned military barracks on Öskjuhlíð. The discovery was made by children playing in the ruins of the former British army command post. The police state that these human remains appear to have been there for a number of months, and a chief inspector declined to comment, other than to say that the case is now being dealt with by CID, who are working on identifying the individual.

Tony turned and faced his mother, who stared blank-eyed into space. He could feel the heat rise to his head. He squeezed his eyes shut as he put a hand over them. After standing still for a moment, he opened his eyes and sat down on the edge of his mother's bed. He pushed a lock of hair away from her face.

'Don't you need a wash, Mum?'

'That would be wonderful,' she said, looking at him beseechingly.

'Mum, listen to me. Do you remember what happened?'

14

Valdimar rang the bell twice and peered through the yellowish frosted glass set in the front door.

He laid a hand on his stomach. He felt a stab of pain and hoped that Ylfa hadn't seen him grimace. They had intended to go straight to Öldugata after going to Baldur's office, but Valdimar suggested stopping off at Askur for lunch.

'Don't you need to be careful, with your arteries?' Ylfa said, expecting a brusque response.

'They do soup and salad,' he'd replied, while mentally mourning their deep-fried chicken.

'She could be at work,' Valdimar said as he tried to distract himself from the pain in his middle, and glanced at his watch, seeing that it was close to two o'clock. He looked along Öldugata. It was a clear day, but bitterly cold, and sunbeams played on the street's imposing houses.

'We can come back later,' Ylfa said, turning to go just as Tony opened the door. Valdimar was startled as a cat shot out through the door and between his feet.

'Good day,' Valdimar said, and introduced himself and Ylfa. 'Can we come inside?'

Tony surveyed them for a moment before opening the door and showing them inside. He shut it behind them, went to the living room and showed them in.

Valdimar looked around the neat, bright living room. On his way along the corridor he had glanced into the kitchen where he saw a mop and bucket, a bottle of cleaning fluid and other items that explained the strong lemon aroma in the air.

'What can I do for you?' Tony asked when they had sat down on the sofa.

'We'd like to have a chat with your mother. Is she at home?' Valdimar asked.

'She's sleeping. She's an invalid ... cancer,' Tony said with a downcast look on his face. 'Can I ask why you want to speak to her?'

Valdimar cleared his throat and shifted forward to sit on the edge of the sofa. He thought before speaking.

'I don't know if you were aware, but a body was found on Öskjuhlíð yesterday.'

'It was on the lunchtime news,' Tony said, also inching closer to the edge of his seat as he faced them. 'Have you found out who it is?'

'Yes,' he said, drawing out the word. 'And that's why we're here. Anything that comes to mind?'

'No. Why should it?'

'It's a man called John Michael Antonelli. Is that name familiar to you?'

'It certainly is,' Tony said after a long pause. 'He is... He was my father. But hold on... That's not possible. He lost his life in the air crash up on Hofsjökull.'

15

Tony knew when he heard the announcement on the radio of the body's discovery that he wouldn't have much time. It wouldn't take the police long to link John with the house on Öldugata, and they could come knocking at any moment. He pushed the wheelchair into the bathroom, undressed his mother and helped her into the bathtub. He washed her hair and sponged her down, dressed her in a thin white nightgown and put her back to bed.

In the kitchen he fetched the tablets and was about to crush them, when he stopped. The usual dose left her very slow and confused. He decided on a smaller dose and mixed it into some orange juice.

'Mum, now you need to listen carefully,' he said, sitting on the edge of the bed. 'You know perfectly well that we haven't seen Dad for a really long time. Isn't that right?'

'Yes, I know all about it,' she said placidly.

'Right. When was that?'

'Well, what? A few months ago.'

'No, Mum. We've been through this again and again. We haven't seen him for four years. That was when he came to see us. That was four years ago,' he said gently, emphasising the number. 'You have to...'

'Yes, but it wasn't that long ago...'

'I know, Mum. It's unbelievable how time flies. It's been four years. You dream about him sometimes,' he lied. 'Sometimes you have dreams that you think are real. But they're only dreams,' he said and stroked her cheek. 'How long has it been since we saw him last?'

'Four years.'

'That's it, Mum. Four years,' he said, kissed her forehead and stood up.

'Why are you so good to me?' she asked gently as he stood in the bedroom doorway and looked down at her.

Her eyes closed and she fell asleep.

'Just today, Mum. Just today,' he said and pulled the door shut.

He went into the kitchen and glanced at the walls. His breathing came fast. *No, I've been over this hundreds of times*, he thought.

He hurried to the living room, parted the curtains and opened the windows wide. He looked out and checked in every direction, before getting out cleaning things. He scrubbed the living room floor, put the sofa and chairs back in their place, wiped down the table, shelves and cupboards.

Yes, check that as well, he thought as he finished with the living room and started on the kitchen floor. He ran a damp rag along the fascia panels under the kitchen units. He got down on all fours and pressed the cloth hard into the channels between the floor tiles.

He was about to wipe down the legs of the table and chairs when the doorbell rang.

*

'It's a pretty big house,' Ylfa said. 'The two of you live here?' Tony looked back at her. He said nothing. 'You and your mother?' she continued.

'Yes. Yes, that's right.'

'Sorry to hear about the cancer. Is it long since she was diagnosed?' Valdimar said, standing up and sauntering around the room. He picked up the only photograph on display, showing a young woman with a baby in her arms. 'I take it this is you and your mother?' he asked, turning the picture towards Tony.

'Yes.'

'When did you last see your father?' he asked, replacing the photograph where it belonged.

'I don't recall. At any rate, it was years ago.'

'He wasn't in touch with you?' Valdimar looked up at a heavy inlaid wooden sideboard that stood against one wall. Such items were nothing unusual in Iceland but were becoming less common with the arrival of flatpack furniture. Valdimar's father had been a handyman and had made exactly such a sideboard that now graced his living room.

'No.'

'He didn't contact you when he was here in Iceland?' Valdimar continued, noticing a bundle of papers on top of the sideboard.

'Excuse me, but I'm going to make some coffee for you,' Tony said, standing up as he saw Valdimar's hand heading for the papers.

'No, please don't. No need for that,' Valdimar said, retreating back to the sofa. His eyes rested on Tony, and he allowed the silence to gather before he continued. 'And? He didn't get in touch?'

'No, we weren't in...'

'Tony, my dear,' a voice called from the bedroom.

'I'll check on her,' Tony said after hesitating, and was startled as Valdimar extended a hand and caught his arm.

'We ought to have a chat with her.'

They looked into each other's eyes for a moment before Valdimar released his grip and Tony went to the bedroom.

'What do you make of it?' Valdimar murmured.

'I don't know,' Ylfa said. 'He comes across as fairly normal. Maybe he's in shock after what you told him.'

'Yes, could be. All the same, he hasn't asked for any

details about what happened to his father. He must know that we know more about this than the little bit that was on the news,' Valdimar said, and was about to say more when they heard a squeak and Tony wheeled his mother in a wheelchair into the room.

He placed the wheelchair at the end of the table and took a seat next to it.

'Good day,' Gunnhildur said, looking at them both.

'Hello, Gunnhildur,' Ylfa said, and introduced herself and Valdimar. 'Perhaps you know why we are here?'

'No,' she said in a dull voice.

'She's quite poorly. I'm not sure this is a good...'

'I'd like to ask, Gunnhildur,' Valdimar said, gently but firmly.

'When did you last see John?'

'John?' she asked, returning his gaze with surprise.

'Yes. The father of your son.'

She looked down at the floor, as if the answer was to be found there. The silence hung in the air for a long time, and Valdimar was about to repeat the question when Gunnhildur looked up. She looked at all of them in turn and opened her mouth.

'It was just... It was just a while...'

'I can see she's not feeling herself,' Tony said and stood up. 'It was just a few...'

16

'What?' Valdimar demanded, sounding annoyed as they sat in the Saab, which still hadn't started.

'Nothing,' she smiled.

She simply had a feeling of wellbeing. They had left Gunnhildur and Tony and as they walked along Öldugata towards the car, Ylfa had hooked her arm into Valdimar's after she had narrowly avoided slipping on one of the icy patches on the pavement. She thought of her boyfriend. It was a long time since she had taken his arm as they walked. She felt that he tended to walk either slightly ahead or a little behind her. He had been irritable recently; or even a little more than just irritable. In fact he had been sulking. Maybe he had a good reason to.

Ylfa had worked long hours, taken extra shifts and evening callouts. All that had increased once she had joined CID. For some reason, she had expected to be doing more daytime shifts, but it didn't turn out that way. It had often fallen to the boyfriend to look after their eleven-month-old daughter, with whom she should have been establishing bonds. Postnatal depression had taken its toll and she felt a gnawing guilt at the relief that came with going back to work. She was well aware that her boyfriend had made real efforts when it came to childcare. He was self-employed and it was easier for him to adjust his working hours. It also didn't do any harm that he had an exceptionally accommodating mother who frequently helped out.

THE DANCER

Last night he had been sitting in silence in the living room when she came in from work. She pulled herself together and baked a sand cake, something with some symbolism for them as a couple.

They had first met in a bakery. They had been side by side at the counter, both of them asking for sand cake. When they met again, at the same bakery, there was no turning back. They chatted and agreed to a date. They called themselves the sand cake couple.

As last night's cake was ready and she was about to take him a slice and a glass of cold milk, he had already gone to bed.

'Everything all right?' Valdimar asked cautiously, taking a moment's break from trying to get the car to start.

'Yes. Why do you ask?' she said in surprise, startled from her thoughts.

'Well, you had a smile on your face just a minute ago and now you look like you've seen a ghost.'

'Ach. It's nothing,' she sighed. She tried to smile, but it was too forced. 'What did you make of those two?'

'Hard to tell. It was barely possible to talk to Gunnhildur, and the lad was somehow... he was reserved as well.'

'Yes. Agreed. There's something odd about the whole affair,' she said, just as Valdimar turned the key and this time the car burst into life.

Valdimar looked at Ylfa as if this were a great triumph on his part, and they set off.

17

'I'm hungry,' she said.

'I'll get something to eat,' Tony said, finally appearing in her bedroom in answer to her endless entreaties.

It was almost nine in the evening, and he wondered where the time had gone. He must have fallen asleep in the chair.

'Are those people gone, Tony?'

'They are,' he said, drawing the curtains more securely together as he noticed how the yellow glow of the street lights slipped through the gap to shine on her face.

He sat on the edge of the bed and looked down at the business card Ylfa had handed to his mother with words to the effect that she should call if she were to recall anything more.

She had fallen asleep in the wheelchair in the living room just as Valdimar and Ylfa were leaving, saying that they would be in touch again.

In touch again. In touch again. What the hell for? He thought. Of course he knew the answer. They didn't appear to be satisfied.

Once they had gone, he had put his mother to bed, where she had lain the whole day long. Tony hadn't responded to her calls, which filtered through to the living room at intervals. He had meant to go back to his place in the shed but hadn't been able to prise himself out of the chair. Not that he really wanted to go back to that wretched shack. It had been a spur-of-the-moment decision to rent it. He had a whole floor of the house on Öldugata to himself. But it was his mother's constant calls that had tipped the balance. They had become so persistent in his thoughts that he could hear them all through the night; even in his dreams, and even when he was walking downtown. He had to escape. He had to find a refuge that nobody knew about. Not his mother, and not his grandfather. Nobody at all.

He had a thundering headache, and his confused thoughts swept here and there in his head like a tornado and there seemed no way to make sense of them. He hadn't even felt pangs of hunger.

Tony started, staring at his mother as if jerked from a dream.

'What were they doing here?' she said and slapped her forehead several times with the flat of her hand. The impression was that her thoughts were an old television that needed a few bangs to shake the picture out of it.

'They were asking about Dad.'

'Why? Where is he?' she demanded in surprise, trying to haul herself to sit upright.

'I don't know, Mum,' he said after a moment's pause, and sighed silently.

He wondered how damaged his mother's mind could be, how few brain cells she had left and how lonely they must be. He knew that she had brought this on herself over the years. He also knew that he had done nothing to help ensure that they would replicate themselves, that they would be renewed. He wasn't sure if the brain had the capacity to renew damaged cells or to generate new ones. But he knew that he was going to slowly but surely ensure that they became even fewer.

With heavy feet, he made his way to the kitchen and looked around. He noticed a tiny dark patch on the ceiling, next to the light fitting. He picked up a cloth and pulled a chair over. He was about to step up onto the kitchen table when the doorbell rang.

He stood motionless on the chair for a while before making his unwilling way to the door. He wondered if it were them returning.

He felt his heart hammering, and it increased as the bell rang a second time.

He opened the door cautiously and stared at the face in front of him.

'What are you doing here?'

THE DANCER

18

Ylfa parked outside her place on Hvassaleiti.

She had gone with Valdimar to the station, where they went through the case files, made calls, sent faxes and quizzed Ævar, who had little to say, but promised more information on the body in the morning.

She looked up at the four-storey block where there were lights in most of the windows. The residents hadn't been able to reach an agreement on the Christmas lights that festooned the handrails of the balconies, still less on the window lights in every colour of the rainbow, some of them flashing. There was one row of windows in the flat on the top floor but one that stood out.

All the lights were off.

There were no Christmas lights.

She opened the door to the flat and clicked on the light in the hall.

When she had taken off her coat and gone into the kitchen, she had seen the note.

Staying with Mum for a while. Steinthór.

She dropped into the chair next to the phone table. She stared at the note in her fingers. The message hit her hard and she could feel her breathing going awry. It wasn't just the fact that he had gone with their daughter, and that they would possibly be away for a few days, but those few days could mean forever.

They had made a habit of leaving notes for each other,

which without exception were signed off with three hearts or an XXX. There was nothing of that kind to be seen on this note. She even turned it over to check the back. He had left that out. The worst of it was that he had signed it off as *Steinthór*. Looking at the name now, she realised how distant this was, so impersonal and bland. He had always signed his notes to her as *Steini*.

She knew that they wouldn't be coming home any time soon.

19

Valdimar entered the silent apartment. After putting his coat on a hanger, looping his scarf, perfectly straight, around the hook and hanging them up, he went into the living room where Ásta was asleep on the sofa. He stood looking down at her for a moment and smiled as she muttered in her sleep as he gently tucked the blanket up to her chin.

Glancing at his watch and seeing it was almost nine o'clock, Valdimar was relieved that he would be able to catch the evening news bulletin. He was about to switch on the radio, and hesitated. He didn't want to wake Ásta. There was a smell of boiled haddock in the air, and he went to the kitchen. He opened the microwave oven and took out a plate on which lay two fillets and four potatoes. Valdimar turned dials after staring at them in confusion and opened the door that gave a familiar squeak.

'Aren't you going to warm it up in the microwave?' Ásta asked, sitting up and looking over the back of the sofa into the kitchen.

'No, my love. You know what I think about that radioactive gubbins.'

'Valdi, it's not radioactive. It's just new technology and it's completely harmless,' she said, standing up and joining him in the kitchen. 'You have to accept new stuff. Here, give me that.'

She took the plate from him and put it inside the

microwave. Valdimar sat at the table and rubbed his face.

'How did it go today?' she asked, sitting down facing him.

'I really couldn't say. Practically no progress. We met the mother and son who are connected to this John,' he said, and explained the connections.

'Isn't it unlikely that they're connected to his death? The woman's sick, and the young lad's hardly going to murder his own father.'

'No,' he said with a smile. He liked it when she took an interest in the questions facing him, although he felt that she could be inclined to jump to conclusions. 'Of course, I don't know anything about the lad. He may have been caught up in something fishy. But there are others who could have an involvement,' he said as the microwave called attention to itself. 'I was in touch with Baldur again...' he said and fell silent as he put a piece of fish in his mouth and waved his hands in the air.

'Baldur the freemason?' Ásta asked, jumping to her feet to fill a glass with water, which Valdimar gulped down.

'That's another reason I can't stand cooking with that wave, micro-whatever. It's still cooking when it's on your plate. Yes, Baldur the mason. It turns out that he deals with John's assets here in Iceland. Baldur said that one of the tenants in the office block on Ármúli is two years behind on his rent and there's a hefty debt there. John also had some land in Mjóafjörður and there have been some disputes over the boundaries. That needs to be looked into as well.'

'And there's that pilot,' Ásta said, and yawned.

'Which pilot?'

'Well, the one who lost his life in the crash on Hofsjökull. Could he have done John some harm? There could be some disagreement there. You haven't checked him out yet.'

'Yes. That's quite right,' he said, and hesitatingly took another morsel of fish.

20

'You don't look very pleased to see me,' Oddur said, grinning as he stood on the steps of the house in Öldugata where he had rung the bell.

Tony was unnerved, and went outside, pulling the door half-closed behind him.

'No... Well, I don't understand. How did you know where I... live?'

Oddur put a hand into his pocket and handed him a scrap of paper.

'This must have fallen out of your trouser pocket when you got changed.'

Tony took the piece of paper. It was a credit receipt from Tómas the Butcher, which had been given a few days before when he returned some spoiled beef. The man had followed the rules to the letter in filling it in, including Tony's name and address.

Oddur took a step closer to him.

'I wanted to see you,' he said, and Tony could smell the booze. 'I mean, we were all worried about you after you disappeared from the practice session. We've never seen anyone dance with that kind of energy... and passion,' he said, his voice voluble and animated.

'Shh. Keep it down,' Tony said, pulling the door more closed. Oddur moved even closer.

'I don't know anything more. But when I saw you dance, well... something happened inside me. I felt I didn't know anything but wanted to know everything. Tony, where did you learn to dance like that?'

Tony didn't reply. He didn't know how to deal with Oddur's proximity. He could smell him; a mixture of sourness and sweetness.

'You must come back to the class. You just have to.'

'I don't know. I...'

He was stopped in his tracks as Oddur kissed him on the mouth.

Their eyes met for a moment, and Oddur cautiously kissed him again. This time it was longer. There was a heat to the kiss, intimate and deep.

When Tony felt a hand slip under his shirt and reach up to his shoulder blades, he pushed Oddur away.

'Sorry! I wasn't going to... Well, yes I was. Just couldn't keep it to myself,' Oddur said with an embarrassed laugh.

'It's all right,' Tony said, breathing hard. He stared into Oddur's eyes. He opened his mouth and was about to speak, when Oddur continued.

'Hey, I really came to tell you that there's a party at Davíð's place. He lives just round the corner and afterwards we're going on to Broadway. Hulda scored some free tickets. Björgvin Halldórs and Helga Möller are playing,' he said, handing him a ticket. 'I promised them you'd come.'

'No,' Tony muttered. 'I can't.'

'Come on. It'll be fun. You'll get to know the crowd better. They all want to meet you, get to know you. He's at Ásvallagata 93, basement flat. Come on over,' Oddur said, again coming closer.

'No, I can't. I have to...' Their lips almost met again. 'I have to go,' he said, stepping inside and shutting the door.

21

Tony parked the van on Álfabakki, not too far from Broadway.

After the conversation with Oddur had been brought to an abrupt end, he had paced the floor as he tried to think through what had happened. He looked at the free ticket, for the sixth time.

His mother called ceaselessly, demanding food. He heated what was left of the stew, which was starting to smell pretty bad by now. He had sniffed the pot when he took it out of the fridge, and it felt as if a chunk of seal meat had assaulted his nostrils. His mother was hardly in any condition to complain, and after he had fed her and put her to bed, he made for the door. He stood on the steps outside for a good while, thinking over what he should do next. He rummaged in the pocket of his jacket for the van keys.

He walked to the corner of Lindargata and Vitastígur where he caught sight of his grandfather's brown van where he had left it, where he had given up on it. Tony was surprised that it was still there, considering it was half on the street and halfway across the pavement. The weather was taking a turn for the worse, although it could have been because of the snow blown from the roofs of nearby houses that had the ability to squeeze into the narrowest crevice and was right now making itself felt against his back. It was so cold that the key refused to go into the lock, so he had to blow on it. He took care to wipe the lock clean of moisture with his jacket sleeve so his lips wouldn't freeze fast to the metal. When he had managed to open the door, he found a scraper and cleared snow and ice from the windscreen. He sat behind the wheel, fully expecting that a divine miracle would be needed for the engine to start. He had no idea what powers were at work, but the van burst into life as if it were brand new, apart from the tugboat rumble of the exhaust.

He scraped the inside of the windscreen clear before gingerly setting off to the sound of metal scraping, which told him that the exhaust had come adrift. Once he was on Skúlagata, where there was generally more traffic and which had cleared the worst of the snow on the road, the noise abated. He pondered whether to head for Grettisgata – or Álfabakki. Unconsciously he took the second option.

Tony went through the nightclub's imposing lobby after having placed his ticket in the vast hand of a doorman who ushered him inside and towards the cloakroom. He by-passed it and went straight for the curved staircase, noticing his fingers on the gilded handrail. The chatter and music grew in volume the further he went, and a thick cloud of tobacco smoke assailed his nostrils. He slipped through the milling throng of people. He saw a man laughing out loud, his face twisted out of shape by some artificial delight, a woman who clearly felt she was a better singer than Helga Möller up there on the stage, and a couple arguing over which of them was the more unpleasant.

The dance floor was packed with people jerking in time to the music. After stopping off at the bar to order a soft drink that cost more than three litres of the same stuff in the corner shop, he saw an empty table in one of the alcoves. He looked around in every direction for the dancers, but they were nowhere to be seen. He had been sitting alone for a while and was wondering if he had made the right decision by coming here, sipping his coke, which was watery and bland.

THE DANCER

Tony watched the people around him, who seemed to be of every age group. He realised that his clothes made him stand out, as most people were dressed in their best. There were older ladies in long dresses and high heels. The younger ones glittered, and their stiletto heels were even higher. There were men in pin-striped suits and lads with bootlace ties and the sleeves of their jackets rolled up.

It was just one such who suddenly appeared before his table, looking at him with searching eyes. His longish brown hair was combed back with water, and his jacket looked to be a size or two too small for his barrel chest. The top button at his thick neck was undone.

'It's you, isn't it?' he said cockily, slurring a little, his voice too loud, and sipping from a glass.

Tony looked back. He recognised him instantly but said nothing. This was one of the faces he longed to forget, but had never succeeded.

'Yeah, it's you,' the cocky guy continued. 'Hey, lads, look who's sitting here,' he whooped, calling to his three friends, and gesturing towards Tony so energetically that the contents of his glass spilled.

Tony slowly wiped his face. He had never seen the others before, but he recalled the name of the cocky one. Pétur, better known as Pesi to his friends. *Ballsy Pesi* to those who were in his gang. He had seemed to have dedicated his whole time through junior and secondary school to making Tony's life a misery. Every opportunity to bully or humiliate him had been taken, everything from degrading name-calling to unprovoked violence.

Tony stared into Pesi's face as he stood there by the table. He searched for features but saw nothing. Or did he? Yes, the scar was right there in its place. Tony never knew who it was, but one time when Pesi had crushed him to the ground in the yard of the Landakot school, landing a series of unrelenting blows to his face, someone in the group gathered around them had kicked Pesi in the face. From then on, he had forever blamed Tony for the mark the kick had left, a deep groove that ran from his temple down to the middle of his cheek.

'What? Aren't you going to say anything?' Pétur demanded.

'Sorry. Didn't hear you,' said Tony, who seemed to have fallen into a reverie of his own.

'I was asking if you got that cool outfit from the Salvation Army?' Pétur asked, and his companions yelped with laughter. 'And how's your fanny these days? Boys,' he said, turning to them. 'From the moment I first set eyes on this lady at the Landakot school, he danced around in his mother's tights,' he announced, turning in a theatrical circle with one hand over his head. Then he spread his arms wide so that the contents of his glass again spilled on Tony, who quickly got to his feet, meaning to lunge and grab him, but Pétur was quicker, grabbing a handful of his hair and forcing his head down to the table so that Tony's glass went flying and the coke dripped into his lap. Pétur leaned down and put his face close to Tony's.

'I always wanted to beat you to death, you pansy cunt. Make it as painful as...'

'What the hell are you doing?' a woman's voice demanded. Tony strained to look up and saw Hulda's face.

'Who the hell are you?' Pétur said, releasing his grip on Tony. 'That's none of your business,' she said, moving close to him. 'But you can be on your way before I knee you in the balls,' she continued, and Tony couldn't stop himself from smiling at the sight.

'You're coming with us, pal,' said one of the two bouncers who had appeared on each side of Pétur, holding him by the shoulders and about to march him out when he wrenched himself free.

'What do you think you're doing? Don't you know who I am?'

'No idea,' one of the pair said in a deep voice, trying to

catch hold of him again, but Pétur slapped his hand away.

'I'm the head fucking chef at Naust.'

'Well, you can go and flip burgers there in peace and quiet,' the doorman said with a practised move that put Pétur in a hold he couldn't escape.

Tony heard only fragments of Pétur's foul-mouthed protestations as he was marched up the steps, his companions meekly following.

'What was that all about?' Hulda asked when they had planted themselves on stools at the bar and ordered fresh drinks.

'Don't know,' Tony said, accepting a glass of coke from the barman.

'Aren't you going to dance?' asked Davíð as he rushed over to them, Oddur at his side, and pulled his brown mop to the back of his neck.

'No,' Tony apologised, pointing at the damp patch at the crotch of his trousers.

'That's just sexy,' Oddur said, snaking an arm around his shoulders and fluttering his eyelashes.

'Thanks for that just now,' Tony said to Hulda, watching Davíð and Oddur head back to the dance floor, each having dispatched a quick shot.

'It was nothing. But seriously, who was that wanker?'

'I don't know. Really,' he said as he caught sight of the doubt in Hulda's eyes. 'Just some drunk arsehole. No idea who he is.'

'I felt so much sympathy for you when you left the practice session the other night,' Hulda said after a pause. 'Are you all right?'

Tony smiled. He didn't reply.

'But it's good to see you. Begga talked about you. She wants you to come back.'

'Really?' Tony said with a smile.

'Yes she does. She asked me to get you to come to a session,' she said earnestly. 'Are you up for that?'

'Could be,' he said, his eyes on her. He looked away when he realised that he had been gazing at her too long.

'There's a session on Monday at eight. It would be great if you could get a part in the Christmas show. The guy in the dragon role has been complaining that his feet are sore.'

'Dragon? There's a dragon in this piece?' he asked in surprise.

'Yes, all kinds of beasts,' she laughed. 'You're coming, aren't you?'

'I suppose so,' he replied, almost absently.

'That's wonderful,' she said, reaching out and hugging him. Tony felt the heat rise inside him. The smell of booze and tobacco was no longer overpowering. Now her sweet fragrance filled his senses.

'What are you doing tomorrow?' she asked, relaxing her embrace.

'Tomorrow? Nothing special.'

'Shall we meet up?'

'Sure,' he hesitated. 'When?'

'Let's go for tomorrow evening. I hear Hornið makes fantastic pizzas.'

22

Tony lay awake on the mattress in his dark room.

He had left Hulda at the bar. He told her that he needed to go, gesturing at the damp stain across his crotch. The weather had worsened and there were flurries of snow in every direction. On his way home he couldn't get Pétur out of his mind, that bastard Ballsy Pesi, and he half-expected to be ambushed as he left the car park outside Broadway.

He did see them in the distance, in the wide-open area in front of the club. Pesi was acting up and his companions were struggling to stop him getting behind the wheel of a black Pontiac Thunderbird decorated with a golden eagle on the hood. Before they managed to bundle him into the back seat, Pesi theatrically flicked his cigarette high into the air.

Tony parked the van in an empty spot on Grettisgata. As if in a daze, he went round to the back of the house and straight to the bedroom, where he threw himself on the dirty, evil-smelling mattress that had come with the place. He pulled the thin duvet over himself and turned to face the wall.

He thought of Hulda.

He thought of Oddur.

He thought of Pétur... Ballsy Pesi.

Tony... Tony... Tony... are you all right?

He jumped to his feet. He must have fallen asleep, and his own scream had woken him. He went to the bathroom and looked in the mirror. His hair was wet and matted. The same went for his shirt. He put out his hands, which shook, and took hold of his wrists. He felt that his body was being squeezed in a vice. There seemed to be some beast inside him that was gnawing at his every sinew, every muscle in his body. Looking in the mirror, now he remembered; he had dreamed them all. He groped in his thoughts for the elusive, tattered remnants of the dream. He had been lying on top of Hulda, who had gasped. He remembered the white feathers scattered around her. Then Hulda morphed into Oddur, who screeched as he took him. Tony stared at the sight of his teeth, sharp and bloodstained. He had looked up at the same moment as a masked figure had snarled, rough and low, *I always wanted to beat you to death, you pansy cunt. Make it as painful as...* as he slashed with the knife at his throat. And now his mother's voice echoed in his head, *Tony... Tony... Tony... are you all right?*

He stared at the image in the mirror and squeezed his eyes shut.

'Tony, answer me. Is everything all right?' the voice called out, and someone hammered at the door.

He opened his eyes and went into the corridor. He looked at the door. The heavy knocks were repeated. Tony opened it cautiously and peered out.

'Tony, thank God. I heard a dreadful scream. Are you all right?' his landlady asked, as she shivered in her dressing gown outside the door.

'Yes... Yeah, it's all right. It was just a nightmare. I'm really sorry I woke you up.'

'I was awake anyway. Couldn't sleep for the noise of the wind. I was so worried. I was about to call the police.'

'No, it's all right. Just go back to sleep,' he said, making to shut the door.

'No,' she said, a hand on the door. 'Come upstairs. I'll make you some soup. There,' she said. 'Come on.'

'I can't. There's something I have to do,' he said, closing

the door, aware that he had sounded more hostile than he had intended to.

He went to the four cardboard boxes in a corner of the living room. These were the four that he had brought from Öldugata but had never opened. When he had rooted through two of them, and opened the third to move the contents about, he found what he was searching for: a photocopy of his mother's script. He quickly leafed through it and stopped at one of several detailed drawings his mother had made to decorate the script, showing costume ideas and suggested stage arrangements.

23

The early hours of Sunday, 5th December 1982

The snow had stopped falling, but the wind blew hard, with all the energy that nature could put behind it.

The colours of the houses merged into the single shade of their snow covering. It also seemed to lay a blanket of silence over the city.

A few cars cruised practically deserted streets and occasionally a figure on foot could be seen, now that it was almost four in the morning.

Tony drove along Hverfisgata, where young people spilled out of nightclubs to stumble, erratically and shivering, along the dangerously icy pavements. Some of them seemed to have some sense of direction, while others appeared to have no idea if they were part of this world or another. A scantily dressed young woman with a high-heeled shoe in each hand waved desperately in the hope that Tony would stop and offer her a lift, but he drove past. He felt sorry for the girl and slowed down, and was relieved to see in the mirror that another car had stopped for her.

He turned down Vitastígur and parked in front of the workshop. The wind whined, but the place was silent as he went into the dark workshop and shut the door behind him. He leaned against the door and enjoyed the silence as he breathed in the aroma of teak oil. He switched on the light and watched motes of dust dance in the air.

THE DANCER

Tony placed the script on the coffee table, and when he had peered at the drawings, he quickly went through the workshop and collected everything he expected to need, placing it all on the workbench. He could feel the tension swell inside him as the adrenaline coursed through his veins to overpower the pain that had crawled inside him and nested there, twisting and feeding on his insides.

Before making a start, he fetched the cassette player and the shoe box from the shelf above the workbench and ran a finger over the tape cases he had lined up there. His finger stopped and he put that tape into the machine, pressed play and cranked the volume up to maximum.

The sound of the Rolling Stones boomed through the workshop.

24

Sunday, 5th December 1982

Tony buttered slices of toast as they popped out of the toaster. He put his plate and a glass of milk on the table and went out to the hall to pick up that day's *Morgunblaðið* from where it lay on the mat.

It had been seven that morning when he had finished what he was doing at the workshop, and he had started to feel hungry. On the way home, he decided to stop off at his mother's house on Öldugata, as there was nothing to eat at his place on Grettisgata.

As he sat by the window, he could see the snow ploughs at work clearing the street. The noise of the scoop smashing through the chunks of ice on the tarmac carried to him.

The paper's front page was all foreign news that was of little interest to him. The domestic news was to be found on the back page, and the item devoted to the murder of John Antonelli was the one that caught his attention. When he read that the police were not inclined to comment, he pushed the paper away. No arrests had been made, but developments were expected.

Tony gazed down at the kitchen wall and then the floor. For a moment he was about to crouch down to the level of the fascia under the kitchen units, but he decided not to. He stood up and put his plate in the sink. He put a cloth under the tap to muffle the sound of it dripping and went to the living room to lie down on the sofa. He stared up at the white-painted ceiling.

He closed his eyes.

*

He saw a vision of himself on a Cooper bike. Not that he had ever had one. He'd never had a bicycle. He had been to the dump with Grandad Jón where they had found a rusty purple bike with white handlebars. Shiny tassels hung from them. The white plastic of the long, narrow saddle was split, but Jón fixed that with a few bindings of tape. His happiness and pride gave way to other feelings that had been plaguing Tony. His mother had been drinking for weeks on end. Her thirst for fun seemed to have no end in sight, and nor did the night-time visits by men, along with the accompanying laughter, screams or tears. He saw himself riding along the street. Despite the taped-up saddle, the rusty frame and the creaks and squeaks from the wheels, his joy was complete. It had never been greater, he reflected.

*

Tony opened his eyes as he heard a squeak. It was dark outside. He sat up on the sofa and checked the time. It was past six o'clock. He had promised to meet Hulda at Hornið at seven.

He heard the creaking again, listened and could hear the low sound again. He knew it right away. He got to his feet and looked along the corridor to see that his mother had somehow wrenched herself free of her stupor and got into the wheelchair. She inched forward, stopped by the telephone table, and put the phone in her lap.

Tony went silently towards her and as she had her back

to him, he watched as a trembling finger turned the dial of the phone. One-one-one-six-six.

25

Gunnhildur looked up, startled, as Tony pressed the button to end the call, cautiously grasped the receiver, took it from her feeble grip and put it back in its cradle.

'I didn't know you were here,' she slurred.

'What are you doing, Mum?' he asked, picking Ylfa's business card up from where it lay in her lap.

'I was going to call this woman.'

'Which woman?'

'Well, this one who left the card,' she said, pointing to it. 'I didn't tell them the truth.'

'What was it you said that wasn't true, Mum?' he said, as he pushed her ahead of him into the kitchen. He brought the wheelchair to a halt by the kitchen table, fetched some yoghurt from the fridge and sat by her side. She grimaced and tried to avoid him as he made to put the spoon between her lips. 'You have to eat, Mum. What were you saying? What was it you said that wasn't right?'

'I don't feel right if I don't tell the truth.'

'That's a bit strange,' he said, succeeding in darting the spoon into her mouth. 'You make such a habit of telling untruths. Come on, tell me what you were going to say to the police lady.'

'It wasn't four years ago that I saw John,' she said sharply, opening her mouth as the spoon approached.

'Really?' Tony said, sounding surprised. 'So when did you see him last?' he said and stood up. He poured orange juice into a glass, crushed a couple of tablets and mixed them into it.

'It was just the other day. Anyway, it wasn't four years ago. I've been thinking about this all day, and I remember seeing him a few months ago.'

'Listen, Mum,' he said, the irritation becoming clear in his voice. 'There, all of it.'

He held the glass tight to her mouth so that it was a struggle for her to drink down the contents. When the glass was empty, he banged it down on the table and pushed her in front of him to the bedroom. Arms lifting under her legs and back, he dropped her roughly onto the bed.

'Are you angry, Tony?' she asked sorrowfully.

'No, I'm not angry,' he said and brushed aside a lock of hair from her forehead. 'But this is something we already talked about. You're getting your memories mixed up...'

'No. I remember it so clearly,' she said, placing a hand on his.

'All right,' he said, jerking his hand back. 'Go to sleep.'

'Are you going?' she asked as he left the room, taking the wheelchair with him.

'Yes. I'm meeting a girl. She's a ballerina,' he smiled. He shut the door.

He put on his jacket, opened the front door, and hesitated. He went back inside, unplugged the phone and put it high up on top of the living room sideboard. On his way out, he opened the jar on the windowsill and helped himself to some change.

26

'Ready to order now?'

The waiter sounded impatient. Tony understood why, and this was the third time he had come to the table.

It had been a good feeling to come into this homely place where anything to do with winter, cold and lousy weather, were left outside. He had taken a seat at a corner table and relished the aroma coming from the kitchen.

'Just a little while,' he pleaded. 'She must be here soon...'

Tony was about to explain, but fell silent as the waiter walked away, rolling his eyes as if searching the inside of his skull.

A moment after he had checked the time and saw that Hulda should have been there three-quarters of an hour ago, she made an appearance, marching towards him.

'Hæ,' she said as she sat opposite him. 'I'm so sorry I'm late. I hope you're not upset. But my dad was driving me home and he got the car stuck in the snow.'

'No problem. It's great to see you,' he said, waving to the waiter who came to take their order. 'He's the only one who has been upset,' Tony muttered, jerking his head in the waiter's direction. 'You live here in the city centre?'

'Yes. On Sóleyjargata. You must have seen the house,' she laughed.

Tony was captivated by her tinkling laughter, and her sparkling white teeth.

'How come?' he asked.

'It's the pink house. The pinkest house in town,' she said with emphasis. 'It was Mum's decision. She loves pink and Dad gave way. They own the house and live there as well.'

'I see. You live with them?'

'Yes, and no. I get a bit of a break from them now because I'm living in the basement flat.'

'Understood,' he said and laughed. He hoped he hadn't sounded too clumsy. He didn't feel comfortable. This was his first ever date. He tried to force himself not to stare at her.

There was an awkward pause and from the look on her face it seemed that it was up to him to make conversation. He was trying to think of something to say when the waiter saved him by bringing their food.

'Looks good,' he said with a smile.

'It certainly does. I've wanted to come here for ages,' she said. 'Do you often go out to eat?'

'Yes,' he replied and looked down at his plate, hoping she would fail to notice the lie.

'Oddur said you live on Öldugata. Do you live with your parents?'

Tony was startled when she mentioned Oddur's name. He didn't want to look up from his plate. She would surely notice the flush, and he felt the heat in his cheeks. He couldn't understand his own reactions. He wasn't able to work out the confusing emotions pulling him in every direction when he thought of Oddur, which became even more confused thanks to Hulda.

'Yah. I live with my mother.'

'Oh. Are your Mum and Dad divorced?'

'No,' he said, looking up to meet her eyes. 'Dad died.'

'That's terrible,' she said, reaching for his hand. 'Was he ill, or…?'

'Yes.'

Tony felt the heavy silence couldn't hang in the air for long. 'Maybe you don't like talking about it,' she said gently.

THE DANCER

'No, it's all right. It was a long time ago. I was only small. I don't remember him much.'

He drew a breath and was about to try to shift the conversation in a new direction when she spoke first.

'And what about your Mum?' 'What about her?' he replied. 'What does she do?'

'She's a dancer...'

'Really?' Hulda asked with sudden animation. 'What kind of dancer?'

'She was a dancer,' he said quickly. 'She was a very fine ballerina. But she stopped many years ago after an accident.'

'Oh,' Hulda said quietly, looking down. 'You said she had been good. Will you tell me about her? I mean, if you want to...'

'She danced from a very early age. She was at the same school of dance as you – as us. She was supposed to have been very talented and was in a lot of productions. But she was in an accident when she was just twenty...'

'What happened?' Hulda broke in.

'I don't really know,' he said, looking out of the window with a distant look on his face. 'It's not something she has ever talked about. But she choreographed a complete performance,' he said, more brightly.

'Really? And was it ever performed?'

'No. The accident wiped her out, as dancing was everything to her. She never really recovered and has been an invalid ever since.'

'In what way?'

'I suppose it's called depression. She shut herself away... And I've pretty much taken care of her ever since.'

He could feel Hulda's eyes on him. Her hand again rested on the back of his and he could feel the warmth from her palm.

'So how come you dance so well? I've never seen anyone dance like that,' she said, squeezing his hand a little.

'Mum taught me. Everything I can do, I owe to her. She started teaching me when I was two or three. I remember the sessions and how much fun it was. But after that it got tougher, and I had to dance in school, and stuff like that.'

'I can well imagine it,' Hulda said. 'Ballet isn't easy for guys. I mean, some just take to it but some, like Oddur, get to suffer. I suppose it doesn't help that... you know... he likes boys. You're not that way inclined, are you?' she asked with a broad smile.

'No,' he said, suddenly concerned that he had answered her question too smartly and with too much emphasis. 'No, I'm not one for boys,' he added, softening his tone. He smiled. 'But Mum made sure I trained from A to Z, and she still does. Let's say that we each sort of live for each other. She helps me dance, and I help her through her illness.'

Hulda looked at him thoughtfully.

'I know it sounds strange, but I'm no mummy's boy. Sometimes she can be intolerable, as many mothers can be, and there are times when I could k...' he said, and his voice faded away. Looking out of the window, he fought to keep the tears in check.

'What is it you want?'

'Sometimes I just long to move away somewhere. To be alone, and free.'

'I know just what you mean. Just getting to move down to the basement has given me so much freedom,' she said and laughed. 'Aren't you going to finish your pizza?'

'No, I don't really feel like it. Do you want it?'

'Tony? Is that you?' he heard someone say behind him. He turned to see a familiar face approaching, but wasn't able to place it. 'Don't you recognise me? Doddi. From school,' he said with a smile and an extended hand, flicking his hair to one side. He wore a black leather jacket with a denim waistcoat over it.

'Yes, of course,' Tony said, now able to put face and

name together. He had hardly been able to recognise him with long hair and a beard.

Doddi had been one of the tough guys at school, and he had hung around with the prettiest girls. Tony had never understood why, but Doddi had been one of the few who had behaved well towards him. It had always been Tony's suspicion that Doddi had been the one who had given Pesi the scar on his face.

'What's new, man?' Doddi asked and crouched down next to Tony's chair 'Doing OK, are you?' he said, slapping his shoulder.

'Yeah, more or less,' he said and tried to force a smile. 'Let me introduce you. This is Hulda...' he said and turned to see her chair was empty. 'She must have gone to the restroom,' he said, looking at Doddi in embarrassment.

'That's a posh word for the bog,' Doddi laughed. 'But life's treating you all right? What are you doing these days?'

'I work in a carpentry workshop.'

'Cool.'

'And you? What are you up to?'

'Deckhand on a trawler. It's lousy, but there's loads of money,' he said, rubbing a finger against his thumb. 'Hey, I have to run,' he said, nodding his head to somewhere across the room. 'Can't keep the lady waiting. Good to see you, Tony.'

'And you,' he said and sighed as he turned back to the table. He could feel the pounding of his heart. His thoughts were in turmoil, tangling and tripping over each other. He didn't cope well with the unexpected, as had just happened. He twisted around and looked across the room. He could see Doddi was talking about him, as the girl he was with glanced in his direction, just as Hulda appeared. She met his eye as she walked across and sat down.

'Sorry. I was bursting,' she said.

'No problem,' he said, swallowing so hard that he could

feel his throat constrict 'Look... I wanted to give you this,' he said, and handed her the necklace he fished from the pocket of his jacket hung on the back of the chair.

Hulda took it and examined what was in her hand. She looked serious to start with, until a smile appeared and spread across her face as she looked at the tiny, delicately carved cherry wood cross.

She let the gilded chain hang from her fingers while the cross lay in her palm.

'Really? You're giving this to me?' she asked, looking into his eyes. 'It's so beautiful.'

'I made it, I wanted to give it to you.'

Hulda closed her hand around it and leaned forward to kiss him on the lips.

'Are you driving?' she asked.

'Yes.'

'How about we go for a little drive?'

27

'It warms up pretty quickly,' Tony said when he noticed Hulda blow on her hands and rub her palms together as they sat in the cold van. He drove aimlessly through the Thingholt district, down to Hlemmur and from there along Laugavegur and Austurstræti.

Hulda smiled to herself, admiring the pendant that hung from her neck.

'You can dance, and you can make necklaces. Are there any other secret talents?'

'I don't think so. Not unless you count the ability to cook absolutely terrible food,' he said, and they both laughed.

'Where do you learn to do this?' she asked.

'The necklace? My grandfather taught me to make all kinds of things. Big and small. I work for him at his workshop.'

'Is that why there's ... what d'you call it? The teak oil smell in the van?'

'I suppose so,' he said, glancing at his watch. It was half-past nine and he took the turn onto Sóleyjargata.

Without Hulda saying a word, he brought the van to a halt in front of the pink house.

'It really is very pink,' he said, and she laughed.

They sat in silence, until Hulda spoke.

'It was a lovely evening, Tony. I'd love to do this again.'

'I had a great time as well. Thanks for coming out to meet me,' he said with a smile.

'I'm the one saying thanks. Thank you for dinner, and special thanks for the necklace,' she said, holding it tight in one hand. She put the other hand on his leg, leaned over and kissed him; first on the cheek, and once she had gazed for a moment into his eyes, her hand slid to his groin and her lips to his mouth. He felt her warm, moist lips and a rising heat in his head. He felt his erection swell as her tongue played over and inside his lips.

'Bye. See you at training tomorrow,' she said suddenly, and got quickly out of the van. She shut the door behind her but stopped and with one fingertip sketched a heart in the frosty covering of the van's window before she walked away.

Tony watched as she trotted along the side of the house. She glanced back and smiled at him before she disappeared down the steps that led to the basement flat.

He shut his eyes. He didn't want to lose the taste of her lips or the sweet fragrance of her that had enveloped him as she came close to his face. He could feel the heat in his groin. He gingerly put a hand on it. He opened his eyes, looked at the house for a moment, and then at his watch.

He swore silently.

The van's rear end skidded on the slippery road surface as he put his foot down.

He was going to be late.

28

Snow was falling hard through the still air.

The engine was running but the lights of the van were switched off where Tony had parked just along from Naust on Vesturgata. He stared at the restaurant's entrance, waiting for the doors to move. It was difficult to make out faces through the falling snow and body shapes became indistinct outlines, as if shown on a television barely connected to an aerial.

Tony checked his watch, saw it was almost ten-thirty, and decided there was a good chance he had already missed Pesi.

He had meant to be there earlier but could hardly blame himself for being late as his thoughts were still focused on Hulda. He stifled the longing to close his eyes and let his mind return to that moment in front of the house. He could sense the heat and the fragrance.

After leaving the pink house, he drove to the phone company building on Kirkjustræti. There were few people around and he had gone straight to one of the phone boxes at the front of the building. It was a relief to find that the phone book hadn't been shredded or burned, and that the phone receiver was in its place.

Tony stacked coins on top of the phone, flipped through the phone book and found what he was looking for. He dropped a coin into the slot and dialled the number.

'Naust, good evening,' a man's voice answered, and

Tony sighed with relief that it wasn't Pesi on the other end of the phone.

'Evening. Pétur's working there, isn't he?'

'That's right. Who's asking?'

'I'm an old friend and haven't seen him for ages. I live abroad and only just landed... He's working tonight, isn't he?'

'He is.'

'I was hoping to take him by surprise. When does his shift end?'

'Got you. The kitchen closes at ten, and they're half an hour, maybe three-quarters of an hour cleaning up. He should be finished by then. Shall I...?'

'Thanks a lot,' Tony said, and hung up. He stared at the receiver, thinking things over. He started to rub the receiver with the sleeve of his jacket so that it dropped from its cradle and hung by the wire. He took hold of the receiver with his bare hands. After jerking it three times, it came free of the pay phone. He opened the van's side door and threw the receiver inside. Then he took a strong but crude wooden chair he had made during the night. He picked it up and placed it upside down in the passenger seat.

He sat behind the wheel and set off.

Tony saw two people leave the restaurant, lighting up cigarettes once they were outside. He peered, checking to see if Pesi might be one of them. The two of them chatted for a while, and it was only when one of them theatrically flicked his cigarette away that he was sure. Ballsy Pesi.

The pair went in different directions, Pesi going around the corner of Vesturgata into Norðurstígur. Tony waited for a while after he had switched on the lights, set off slowly and turned onto Norðurstígur, where he saw Pesi crouched on his heels next to the Pontiac.

Tony let the van coast gently over and stopped, leaned over to the passenger side and wound down the window.

'Need some help? What? You?'

THE DANCER

'What the fuck are you doing here?' Pesi demanded after peering between the legs of the chair and realising who was offering to help.

'I was on the way past. Looked like there was someone in trouble.'

'Fuck!' he yelled. 'Two flat tyres! That's not possible. You don't get two punctures at once!'

'I'll agree with you on that. It's pretty unbelievable,' Tony said sympathetically. 'There could have been something sharp under the snow when you parked it,' he said, getting out of the van and going over to Pesi. 'And I guess you don't have two spare wheels, do you?'

Pesi flared his nostrils as he glared at Tony, who wouldn't have been surprised to get a punch in the face in return.

'Come on, what are you doing here?' Pesi asked finally.

'I work at a carpentry workshop, and I was delivering a chair to a customer round the corner,' he said, pointing along Geirsgata.

'Must be an important customer.' Pesi lit a cigarette and exhaled a cloud of smoke that was mostly blown back into his face. 'Can you give me a lift home?' he asked with a grimace.

'Sure. Jump in,' Tony said, and made for the driver's door.

'I'm not going to squeeze in next to that thing,' Pesi said, pointing at the chair wedged in the passenger seat.

'Ach, yeah. You'll have to help me move it to the back. It's not light,' he said, and pulled open the passenger door.

Pesi flicked away his cigarette and took hold of the chair. 'It's not that heavy,' he said, lifting it up. 'Open the side door.' Tony slid the side door back and switched on the little light inside that cast a weak brownish glow.

'Sorry about all that shit at Broadway the other night.'

'It's best if you can drop it over there by the door so it won't move.'

Pétur scrambled inside and pushed the chair ahead of him.

'Here?' he asked.

Tony shut the door and Pesi wasn't quick enough to turn around before Tony stabbed the bradawl he had used earlier to puncture his tyres deep into his upper arm. Pétur howled, grabbing at the wound, as Tony stabbed again, this time sinking the spike into his left shoulder.

'What are you doing, man? What's...' Pesi said, and his words were cut off as Tony pushed him back, so that his head connected with one of the van's metal frames, and he slumped down. Tony hauled him upright from where he lay on the floor and rained blows to his face.

Tony lay exhausted on top of Pesi, who lay motionless, his breath coming in irregular gasps. Tony held his breath as he heard a car come to a halt behind the van. He clapped a hand over Pesi's mouth, listening to a conversation, then doors slamming, followed by silence. Tony listened for a long time, got to his feet, and hauled Pesi into a half-upright sitting position. He manoeuvred his head under Pesi's armpit and managed to work the limp body into the chair, where he tied him hand and foot.

'You're not going to bleed to death here,' he gasped as he bandaged the stab wounds tightly. 'You see, I don't want you to die right away, Pesi, Ballsy Pesi. Pesi little balls.'

He opened the side door and peered outside.

'Yeah. I almost forgot. There's no way I could forgive you for that shit at Broadway. I don't forgive you for any of the things you did to me. And that's precisely why you're here right now,' he said, slamming the door shut hard.

THE DANCER

29

Monday, 6th December 1982

The dancers sat in a circle on the stage of the National Theatre. Begga had brought the session to an end after an hour's practice.

'Stop, stop, stop,' she had ordered over the booming music, marching with quick steps to the cassette player to switch it off. 'Stop, stop, stop,' she repeated, just as loudly, even though the music had been turned off. 'Young man. Young man, you can't continue like this,' she said, going over to the dancer who was supposed to be in the role of the dragon.

'I'm all right,' he said feebly.

Tony could see in his eyes that this wasn't true. He had noticed that the lad was in real pain, but with so much at stake, he was clearly unwilling to admit it. He had been unable to keep the pain from his face through the challenging steps and the leaps that the role demanded.

'No, dear boy,' she reproved, trying to soften her tone, something Tony had noticed she only did with difficulty. 'You're going to go and get that foot checked out. Go home now and get someone to take you to hospital. That needs an X-ray.'

The boy did his best to protest, but Begga was adamant. Finally, the lad left the stage in tears.

During the night, Tony had gone straight to Grettisgata

from the workshop and was asleep the moment his head touched the pillow. Waking up around midday, he felt as if a great weight had been lifted from his shoulders. He thought of Hulda and could hardly wait to see her at that evening's training. From the moment he opened his eyes, he was constantly glancing at his watch, and eventually realised that this simply made the time pass even more slowly.

He stepped under the flow of hot water and sat in the shower tray. He opened the flask Hulda had given him and rubbed the oil into his feet, feeling a glow of wellbeing course through him. He realised this when he noticed that he was singing, as if to himself: *Do, do, do, do it...*

Tony dressed and stopped off at Bernhöft's bakery on the way to Öldugata.

'Dearest Mum,' he said as he found her lying on the bedroom floor and fetched the wheelchair. He helped her into it and looked at her thoughtfully for a while. It occurred to him that he had never before called her *Dearest Mum*.

'Time for something to eat.'

'Tony, why are you being so nice to me?' she asked after he had made her a meal and helped her take a bath.

'It's because I'm so happy.'

30

'Tony, are you listening to me?' Begga snapped as she crossed the stage to where the dancers sat in a circle.

He froze, and the image of his mother as he kissed her forehead before leaving the house on Öldugata vanished from his mind.

'There's no point shedding tears, even though we've lost one of our dancers. It's a tough world. We have to be ready to take on setbacks and challenges. Sorrow and joy.'

The dancers looked down at their hands. Tony shot a glance at Hulda. She seemed even more beautiful when she was sad than when she had a smile on her face. He longed for her to look his way.

'Tony,' Begga said, her voice ringing. He looked up at her. 'I know you're new here, but you performed outstandingly today, and managed to stay focused without drifting off into some world of your own,' she said, as her tone softened.

She's right, he thought. He had managed to follow Begga's instructions during the training session without his mind wandering away to the living room at home in the middle of a sequence. He did everything he could to relive the experience at Hornið, the heat of the kiss, her touch on his groin, and his feelings as she drew the heart on the van's frosted window. When his focus was on Hulda, there was no room for his mother in his thoughts.

'You'll take this one,' she said, handing him the script, as the dancers looked at him and then each other. 'You're taking the role of the dragon and you only have a few days to be absolutely certain of what it involves. It's a vital role, but it's short as you only appear in the closing scene. I have every confidence that you can do this, and you can do some extra training in the room upstairs,' she said, and placed a hand on his shoulder.

'Is the session over?' called a voice from the darkened auditorium. 'We have a practice in twenty minutes, and we'll need the stage.'

'Yes. All done,' Begga said, after peering into the darkness, where she made out a director who was rehearsing a play at the theatre. 'That's it, kids. Go home, go over your scripts, and practice. The opening night is on Friday, and we have to be a hundred per cent ready. One hundred per cent,' she said, with additional emphasis. 'Costumes will be ready tomorrow or the next day. I'll see you all here on the stroke of four o'clock,' she said, clapping her hands.

*

'Hæ,' Tony said, going over to where Hulda stood alone on the steps at the side of the National Theatre.

'Hæ,' she said with a faint smile.

'A shame for that guy,' he said, noticing that she looked downcast.

'Yes,' she said, without looking at him.

'Is everything all right?'

'Yes, of course it is,' she replied, as if the question had taken her by surprise.

'It was lovely to see you yesterday. It was fun,' he said after a pause.

'Yes, it was great. A pity about that unpleasantness with whatshisname, Pesi.'

'Oh, that,' Tony laughed. 'That was so weird. And forgotten...

'I meant yesterday,' he continued, glancing shyly at her. 'No necklace? Maybe you didn't like it after all?' he said, stepping closer.

'What are you talking about?' she said, looking up and backing away.

He looked into her eyes, unable to comprehend why he felt that the stone was forcing its way back into his body.

'The necklace. The one I gave you yesterday.'

'Tony, I don't have a clue what you're talking about,' she said, catching his eye. 'Yesterday? What about yesterday? We didn't see each other yesterday,' she said, her chin jutting forward as if to give emphasis to her words.

'Hulda,' he said, looking around in confusion. 'We met at Hornið yesterday... we talked, drove around, and...' he said and reached for her hand.

'What are you doing?' she snapped, jerking her hand back and taking another step back.

Tony moved closer and went to touch her shoulder, but she swatted his hand away.

'Hulda, what's got into you? I thought... I love...' he said and got no further.

Tony managed to put out a hand to break his fall. He looked up to see Davíð's face, as he crouched down, hands clamped around his throat.

'What are you up to?' he snarled, the anger shining from his face. 'What were you thinking? That Hulda's in love with you?' he said as he released his grip and stood up. 'What the fuck made you think that?'

Tony made to get up, but Davíð reached behind his head, grabbed hold of his ponytail and forced Tony's face close to his.

'Leave my girlfriend alone, or I'll kill you.'

'Davíð, please,' Hulda said as he straightened up and landed a kick to Tony's side.

Davíð walked away.

'I don't understand what's got into you, Tony. But this

is just wrong. What on earth makes you think you love me? We don't know each other at all,' she said, with an expression of something close to sorrow on her face as she stooped over him. 'You'll have to pack this in,' she said, smiled fleetingly and went over to Davíð, who put an arm around her as they walked away along Hverfisgata.

31

We didn't see each other yesterday ... We didn't see each other yesterday.

Those words echoed through his head as if there were space in there for nothing else. He paced the living room floor at the house on Öldugata and wanted to not believe what had happened. He tried to banish the endlessly repeated sentence from his thoughts. He longed to catch hold of other thoughts; to put them together in a coherent sequence. But it was like trying to catch bubbles. No sooner he had got hold of one thought, than it would vanish. The same happened with the next... and the next. Then they would reappear, unexpectedly and randomly. They fluttered around inside his head for a moment and disappeared.

Tony dropped to his knees and put his hands to his head, which he thought was going to burst, as if a stone core deep inside him had cracked and was crumbling, spreading through his veins.

He huddled into a ball and howled.

'Is everything all right, Tony?' a voice called from the bedroom.

Tony didn't move.

'Tony! What's the matter? Aren't you going to bring me something to eat?'

He lay still and tried to bring his breathing under control. He managed to shut out his mother's calls. He looked up and stared for a long moment into space.

'It can't be right,' he said to himself, and got quickly to his feet, ran out of the house and along Öldugata to where he had parked the van. He stared at the side window where Hulda had drawn a heart, but there was nothing to be seen. Maybe all the evidence had been wiped away, he thought. He breathed hard on the glass in the hope that the heart would materialise.

Nothing happened.

Tony started the van and took a route leading to Hafnarstræti. He parked hard against the pavement, hauled open the door and hurried into Hornið.

A couple of the customers looked up in surprise as he stood in the doorway and scanned the room.

'Ah, it's you,' said the waiter from the evening before when he noticed Tony. 'Wait a moment,' he said, and disappeared into the kitchen. 'Here, you forgot this when you were here last night,' he said, holding out a hand.

Tony caught the waiter's eye for a moment. Something deep inside wanted to stop him from looking down. He finally dropped his eyes and saw the necklace lying in the man's palm.

32

Tony lay on the sofa in the living room, listening to the tones of Johann Sebastian Bach from the speakers, blended with his mother's calls from the bedroom. To begin with they hadn't been able to fight their way through the music, but gradually they drilled their way into his consciousness and took over.

He got to his feet, turned up the music and picked up the script Begga had given him. He looked at the opening page.

The Dragon
A ballet by Birgitte Stefánsson, 1963

He had hardly sat down again before the cat jumped into his lap, rubbed itself against his arm, then curled up and lay purring in his lap.

Tony stroked the cat as he read through the script. He hadn't gone through many pages when he realised that some of the scenes looked remarkably familiar.

At the practice sessions he hadn't performed the whole work, only odd scenes, so he hadn't realised how the whole thing looked.

He read further and could feel the heat in his face. There wasn't just the dragon, which was supposed to be his role, and which he had taken as a coincidence. There was also the swan, and the wolf, just as in his mother's script. The characters danced, interpreted and performed in exactly the same way. This couldn't be a coincidence, he thought.

'Tony!' his mother screeched. 'You must come, right now!' Tony felt the cat's claws graze his arm and was startled as he looked down and saw only the whites of its eyes. He was shocked to see his hand clenched tight around the animal's neck, and it was close to being choked to death. He quickly relaxed his grip and after a moment the cat scrambled to its feet, jumped to the floor and hissed at him.

He stood up and fetched his mother's script from on top of the sideboard. Then he sat at the kitchen table with the script side by side.

The Dancer
A ballet by Gunnhildur Jónsdóttir, 1965

When he had gone through a few pages, he buried his face in his hands. He wasn't sure if he said it out loud, or silently to himself; *Mum, what have you done?*

'Come on,' he said with determination, marched to the bedroom, lifted her briskly into the wheelchair and wheeled her rapidly in front of him to the kitchen. This time he placed the wheelchair in the middle of the floor.

'Are we eating here?' she asked, trying to look round at him.

'We're not eating anything. It's dance time,' he said, filling her a glass and starting to pull off his clothes.

'No. Tony, no. Don't dance. Not today.'

'Yes, mother. I'm going to dance, and you're going to tell me what you think. You'll tell me what I'm doing wrong, because you never say a word when I get something right.' He untied the knots holding back his hair. 'From the day you started making me dance, naked as that's the way you always wanted it, you have never, not once, given me the slightest praise. You've never told me how good I am. All you have ever done is to scream at me when I get something wrong in this ballet of yours, which you stole.'

He slipped into his ballet shoes.

'What are you talking about, Tony?' she scowled.

'None of that, mother. I've found it all out.' He went to the record player. 'You stole the script. I'm dancing in a role at the National Theatre which is practically identical to your script. The characters are the same, the dance moves are the same. Everything in yours is the same as in Begga's script, which she wrote in 1963, and yours is written in 1965.'

'Begga? Is she...?

He picked up the record player arm.

'Mum, you've been making me dance to this stolen work all these years. My life is one big lie. You're a liar and a thief, Mum,' he yelled, tears flowing down his cheeks.

'Hold on, Tony, This Begga...'

The sudden onslaught of noise from the loudspeakers drowned out her words.

Tony took his position, lifted himself onto his toes, and raised a hand up the line of his body. His hips twisted to one side as he straightened his right leg from his body, which leaned gently aside, and he danced steps around the room and the wheelchair on his toes.

He spun around, his limbs stretching and swaying like a strip of silk in the wind.

His mother tried to speak, turning her head in every direction as he danced around the wheelchair in time with the deafening music.

Tony snatched up a cushion and spun in a circle behind her. With a single quick movement, he placed the cushion over his mother's face. He held it there for a long time.

33

Tuesday, 7th December 1982

'Wouldn't the Saab cope with it?' Ylfa asked with a sly grin as she saw Valdimar panting his way up the slope to where she stood on a level piece of ground half-way up the hillside. She had glanced down earlier, alerted by what had sounded like a chainsaw, to see the Saab fishtailing as Valdimar tried to rev it up the track that meandered upwards. Finally he gave up and walked.

He had just come that morning from the doctor, who had told him in no uncertain terms that he needed to slow down and make some changes to his diet. It was when he arrived at the police station just before midday that he had been told to go straight to Úlfarsfell.

'Why wasn't this one given to someone else?' Valdimar asked, pretending he hadn't heard Ylfa's question.

'Lots of reasons, or so the chief said. Flu, to start with. A murder in Hafnarfjörður, the fatal accident on Reykjanesbraut during the night, and God knows what else.'

'Have you been here long?' he asked looking around.

'No, not really. Forensics have only just started examining the body and the crime scene.'

'Who found it?'

'A man called into the station around eleven. This was found on him,' she said, handing Valdimar a driving licence.

'It was a couple taking a walk as it was getting light, and they came across all this,' she said, gesturing to the chair and the man sitting in it. The body had been covered in snow, which the forensics team had brushed away to reveal the leather mask. One of the technicians photographed the body and its surroundings from every angle.

Valdimar went over the body and looked through the holes in the mask. He found his gaze meeting the wide-open eyes of the person inside. He turned and looked up Úlfarsfell and finally towards the city.

It had snowed unrelentingly through the night, and he admired the beautiful view from here on the hillside over Reykjavík dressed in its sparkling winter best. A farmhouse and a stable stood at the foot of the hill.

'Who chooses a place like this?' he said thoughtfully.

'Good question. He'd have had to pass the farm down there and the stables. We'd better call in there,' Ylfa said.

'Yes, and he must have been driving something a bit more powerful than a Saab.'

'Maybe. But there wasn't much snow here yesterday.'

'How do you know that?'

'The couple who called in are big on walking and come here a few times a week. They were here last night and said there wasn't nearly as much snow then. It didn't start to fall heavily until sometime during the night.'

'I see. And that will have helped the perpetrator. All foot and tyre prints are long gone,' he said, turning back to the body. He examined the chair and the chains. 'Somebody went to a lot of trouble with this.'

'Yes. It must have required a lot of imagination, and effort.'

'Morning,' said Ævar, coming over and extending a hand. 'I have to admit that this is one of the strangest things I've seen in my career.'

'I reckon I have to say the same,' Valdimar said. 'Any ideas of the cause of death?'

'No. We need to get the body back to the morgue. But we need to go over the whole crime scene before we can move it. It's more complicated than usual, and the snow doesn't help us in that respect.'

'Found something!' a voice called from further down the slope.

They looked downhill to where one of the technicians had come across something under the snow. They went over to where he was painstakingly brushing snow from what appeared to be a piece of canvas or a tarpaulin.

Ævar stooped to examine it. He cautiously took hold of one corner and looked closely at some stains on it. Finally he crouched down on all fours and put his face close to it. Then he raised his head and looked straight at Valdimar and Ylfa.

'This stinks of varnish,' he said.

34

'You'll have to give me a hand with this,' his grandfather said as Tony walked in through the workshop door.

Old Jón stood on a rickety wooden stool with a length of wood in his hand, poking at a cardboard box that had been placed on the rafters beneath the high roof.

'Grandad, what are you doing?' Tony asked as he rushed over to grab hold of him around the hips just as he was about to come crashing down. 'You shouldn't be climbing up there like that.'

'What? It's not as if I'm some kind of old man.'

'Yes, exactly, Grandad. You are an old man. Nothing wrong with that, but you have to know your limits.'

'Don't talk such damned rubbish,' Jón rasped in irritation, jabbing with the piece of wood and sending the box flying, so that it landed with a crash on the floor. 'There. Done it.'

Tony helped his grandfather down from the stool and sat with him by the coffee table.

'And what's all that?'

'Well, it's the Christmas decorations. We should put decorations up, don't you think?' he said, glancing around.

Tony was taken by surprise, as he didn't recall his grandfather ever putting up decorations in the workshop before. He wondered what the reason might be. It could hardly be for the benefit of the few customers who came by. He consoled himself with the thought that if this made his grandfather happy, then he'd help him with it.

He himself had never been much of a one for decorations, and there had been plenty of Christmases over the years when nothing of that nature had been seen at home.

'This one must have broken when it dropped,' Tony said, holding up a cracked gilded star.

'No, that one broke many years ago. I've just never had the heart to throw it away,' his grandfather said, taking it reverently from Tony's hands. 'This was a present from one of my best customers. Anyway, are you all right, Tony? Seen a spook, have you?' he said, patting his leg fondly.

'Seen a what?'

'A ghost? You look so pale.'

'I'm fine. Just a bit tired,' Tony said, looking away.

They took things from the box for a while without saying a word.

'Grandad,' Tony said in a subdued tone as he took out a tangled string of lights.

'Look, we can use this one,' his grandfather said happily, holding a candle with a calendar on it that had burned down to the number five.

'Grandad, there's something I want to ask you.'

'And what's that, dear boy?'

'Why didn't you... don't you and Mum get on? Did something happen?'

'We can put this one on the door,' Jón said absently, holding a battered Christmas wreath with red ribbons and two pine cones.

'We need to talk about this, Grandad. What happened?'

Jón reached for the coffee pot and poured himself a cup. 'Well, I don't know,' he said, hunched forward, the cup cradled in both hands. 'I'd have preferred to spare you all that.' He stared blankly ahead.

'From what?'

'She could never bring herself to forgive me,' he said

with a sigh. 'It was the Spring of 1955. She was twenty-three and my little darling was doing so well. She was completely captivated by dancing, and at that time she was seen as one of Iceland's leading talents, and with good reason. She had been offered an audition in America.' A dreamy look appeared on his face. 'Let's say that fateful decision on my part was what turned her life upside-down.'

'What do you mean by a fateful decision?'

'To take her with me.'

35

May 1955

'Are you sure this is all right, Dad?'

'Yes, of course it is, sweetheart,' he said, and waited for her as they made their way up Hengill's steep slope.

It was a windless, beautiful day. Scattered white clouds could be seen in the distance, and they appeared motionless, high in the sky.

'But Mum said this could be dangerous. I'm not sure I want to go any further,' she said as she gave up trying to clamber over a boulder that blocked her path.

Jón made his way back, took her hand and hauled her to him.

'You know what your mother's like. She's frightened of everything. I've always said that she's over–protective of you,' he said as they continued up the slope. 'I want you to live life, Gunnhildur. There's so much more in life than dancing.'

'But that's the only thing I can do. It's the only thing I love, and I don't want...'

'Yes, I know that perfectly well, and I support you wholeheartedly. But I don't understand why you should exclude everything else...'

They made their way up the steep slope of the mountain, made up of broad rocky outcrops, escarpments and crags. Along their route, the terrain ranged from large rocks to fine scree that could slip from beneath their feet.

'Look how beautiful it is,' Jón said when they finally stood on the edge of the precipice and admired the view that stretched away in every direction.

The route had been on the sheltered side of the mountain, but up here on the bare peak, the wind blew unhindered and with much greater force.

'Shouldn't we be heading back?' Gunnhildur asked, pulling her hat down to better cover her head.

'No, we're not quite there yet,' Jón said in an encouraging tone, sending her a smile.

'Not there? What do you mean?' she asked in surprise.

'That's where we're going,' he said, pointing at the highest peak. 'We're going to conquer Skeggi.'

'Dad, I can't go any further,' she said as they had hiked in silence all the way to Skeggi and had started the trek upwards.

'This is something you'll never regret. Once we're up there we'll have a view over Mosfellsheiði, Hellisheiði, the Thingvellir Lake and so much more. We'll stop for a bite to eat when we're up there.'

36

'Of course, I should never have taken her up there,' Jón said, putting his cup aside with trembling hands. He tapped the snuff tin against the back of his hand to leave a mound there.

Tony could see the anguish in his eyes.

'Did something happen, Grandad?'

'We were making good progress up Skeggi. Even though she protested, she was tough and put her back into it. I wanted to show her, and give her the achievement of reaching the pinnacle, even if it was only Hvannadalshnjúkur,' he said, passing his hand under his nose and snorting the snuff in a single movement. 'Then down came the fog, as if a wand had been waved. In a moment, you could hardly see your hand in front of your face. I wanted to get down quickly, and we held onto each other. But that wasn't always possible when we had to clamber over the largest rocks. I went ahead so I could help her down, and then...'

'And then, what, Grandad?'

'She didn't follow behind me. I lost her,' he said, and dissolved into tears.

Tony put out a hand and rubbed the old man's shoulders.

'I can never forgive myself. I called and called, but there was no reply. I've no idea how long I walked, searching for her. It's a complete mystery to me, but of course the Almighty had a hand in this, and I simply came across her,' he said with a sigh.

'And what?' Tony asked after a long silence as Jón had hunched forward in his chair, his face buried in his hands.

'Fog plays tricks on your hearing. She went in the wrong direction when I called out to her. When I finally found her, she had tumbled over quite a high cliff and was lying at the bottom, motionless. I thought she was dead. I sat with her for a long time until the fog lifted. It was such a relief when I saw some other hikers and they helped me bring her down. It turned out that her leg was badly broken.'

'And she could never forgive you for that,' Tony said thoughtfully, his chin resting on his fist.

'No. That she never did, and nor could anyone blame her for that. But it wrecked her dreams of a future as a dancer. And she was right. Dance was everything to her, and the only thing she knew. There was nothing else ahead of her,' he said and stood up, having already picked up the decorations, packed them away in the box and closed the lid.

'It's not as if you didn't make an effort to make up with her, Grandad. I know what you've tried to do for Mum. Always ready to help and support her.'

'Yes,' he said slowly. 'That's as may be. But she'd never accept any help. After that her life was on a downward slope. We both know how that turned out. You, Tony, hardly know anything else.'

'You've done your best for me as well.'

'She made another attempt to apply for the dance academy. Did you know that?' Jón said and looked over to where Tony stood by the lathe.

'No. I wasn't aware of that.'

'The doctors said that she'd never dance again. But with unbelievable perseverance and hard work, she made a recovery. She was completely ready and applied.'

'And what?' Tony asked in excitement.

'She was turned down,' Jón said, brushing dust and wood

shavings from the bench.

'Why?'

'It's hard to tell. They just wouldn't accept her. You know she choreographed a ballet?'

'Yes... I know something about that,' Tony said hesitatingly.

'She sent that to the National Theatre, and that was rejected as well. She gave your grandmother a copy and I read it, and it was a fine piece of work. There was plenty of darkness in there, but it was still excellent.' Tony could hear the pride in his grandfather's voice. 'I took it on myself to go down there myself and talk to some of the jobsworths at the National Theatre in the hope of making them see sense. But it was like trying to talk to the wall. There's one down there I'll always remember because she was downright rude,' he said pensively.

'Really?' Tony asked.

'That's right. She said she'd never seen such rubbish in her life. I suspect this was the same woman who prevented her from applying again for the dance academy. Y'know, you're looking mighty pale, Tony. Won't you have a cup of coffee to perk you up?' he asked, hovering to fill a cup for him as well as his own.

'I don't think so. No thanks.'

'All right, then,' he said and sat down. 'I recall that she once went to your house on Öldugata.'

'Who?'

'This woman who turned your mother down.' 'What?' Tony asked, standing completely still.

'Well, you must have been nine or ten. You had been dancing at school and must have made an impression, because someone got in touch with the dance academy, and she and another woman turned up at your house.'

'And what were they after?' Tony asked, feeling the rage churn inside him, certain already that this wasn't going to be a pleasant tale.

'They wanted you to attend the academy. Unusually, and to my amazement, your mother had accepted my help in fixing a water leak in the kitchen. That's how it happened that I was there,' Jón said, dipping a sugar lump into his coffee and putting it in his mouth.

'I was always so sorry that their visit ended the way it did. I think your mother suffered some kind of breakdown on the spot when she saw who was standing there on her doorstep. Once she had listened to all the compliments intended for you, all her own anger boiled over and I thought she was about to break both of their noses as she slammed the door...' he said, and was interrupted by an ostentatious sneeze, and blew his nose.

'Take it easy, Grandad.'

'What? Where was I? Yes, I think your mother had a bitter hatred for that woman... What the hell was her name? Ach, she was a proper snooty cow.' He put a hand to his forehead and rubbed it back and forth, as if that would stimulate his memory. 'Bogga,' he said loud and clear, his index finger in the air. 'She was called Bogga.'

'You mean Begga?' Tony said, getting to his feet.

'Yes, you're right. It was Begga. She had a thick German accent.'

37

'It's all coming together and I'm truly proud of you,' Begga said when they had performed part of the piece. 'Sit down and listen.'

The group sat on the stage and Tony took care to not sit anywhere near Hulda and Davíð, who had glared at him a few times during the practice session. He had glanced in Hulda's direction at the same moment and felt a relief to see what looked like a faint smile. It could have been his imagination, he thought. Yes, he decided. It had to be a mirage.

'A little quiet, please,' Begga demanded as the chatter in the group magnified. 'You know the first night is on Saturday. Today's Tuesday and we don't have access to the auditorium again until Friday for the last rehearsal...' she said and there was a collective groan. 'Yes, yes. I know. Unfortunately, we don't have any more practice opportunities this week because we're not the only ones rehearsing performances here. You all have pretty much everything clear, but all the same, I'd like to have some of you come for an extra rehearsal upstairs.'

She named some of the group, including Oddur and Davíð, who, judging by the look on his face, wasn't impressed.

Tony looked out into the auditorium when he saw lights appear for a moment in the otherwise darkened space. Two figures came in through the door at the top right-hand corner, shutting it behind them. He saw only their dim outlines as they stood and appeared to be watching.

'But, I'm pleased to say that...' Begga continued, after stepping backstage for a moment and returning, pushing a long clothes rack ahead of her. 'Tan-tan-ta-ra! The costumes have arrived!'

Some of the dancers were instantly on their feet in delight, crowding around the rack as they searched for their costumes. Others remained relaxed.

Begga had again gone backstage to fetch a smaller rack, and she called Hulda, Davíð, Oddur and Tony over to her.

Tony stayed on the floor and watched as Begga handed Oddur a dark brown, furry overall. This came with a wolf mask that he pulled over his head and began whining and growling, so that those around him dissolved into laughter.

'You can keep it for the performance, Oddur. You're a wolf, not some pussy cat,' she laughed. 'We'll go over all this again,' she said, and turned to Hulda and Davíð. 'You two are the beautiful pair of swans,' Begga said in unmistakeable delight as she handed them each a pair of pure white wings and head coverings in the same colour. 'There are a few things we need to go through, Davíð. Your timing against the music needs to be better, as this has to be absolutely precise. We also need to look at the pirouettes, you know. Rapid turns. You're the male bird, Davíð. Dignity and brilliance are all-important.'

'Should I bite your neck?' Oddur said in a low growl in Tony's ear, startling him. 'Are you busy after the practice?'

He took off his mask and grinned.

'No. Why...?' Tony asked in surprise.

'Just... In case you wanted to...' he said, but Begga broke in, calling Tony over.

'Your costume, Tony,' she said, a broad smile on her face. Tony took it and looked at what she had given him. He had half-expected something more adventurous than this, which had turned out to be a dark grey all-in-one suit made in rough material, with a matching mask, all of which seemed to him to be rather juvenile.

'Don't you think it's great?' she said in admiration. 'Aren't you going to try it on?'

'Maybe later,' he said, looking away as he was concerned she would sense his disappointment.

'Is everything all right, Tony? I noticed during the practice that you were a little distant. Don't you feel well?'

'Everything's fine,' he said after a pause.

'Fine. I have to say, you performed wonderfully at the rehearsal. You have a unique talent, Tony, and you've clearly rehearsed thoroughly,' she said seriously, pacing a hand on his shoulder.

Her praise gave him something of a warm feeling inside, but at the same time he wanted to tell her that he had been rehearsing this part for the last seventeen years.

'Well, rehearsal is over, and we'll meet...' she said, and fell silent as two strangers approached.

'Good evening. We're from CID. My name is Valdimar, and this is Ylfa.'

They both had their eyes firmly on Tony.

38

'Let's make a start, shall we?' Valdimar said, looking up at the clock on the office wall, which told him that the four of them had so far spent an hour waiting, each in an interview room.

'Yes, I think so,' Ylfa said, also glancing at the clock. 'It'll be interesting to hear what happened at Broadway.'

'Is it all right if you talk to Hulda and Davíð? I'll take Tony and Oddur,' Valdimar said, rising to his feet.

'Sounds good.'

Valdimar and Ylfa had already interviewed Pétur's friends who had been with him at the nightclub. All of them had alibis that had been confirmed.

They had called in at Naust and chatted with Pétur's manager and others who worked at the restaurant. Most of them had reported that he had been a hard worker, likeable and cheerful, but that would change when he had a drink. Then he would have trouble keeping his temper in check. One of the staff stated that Pétur had been dealing drugs on a small scale but wasn't aware that he used them himself. This member of staff knew that Pétur had gone with a group of friends to Broadway on Saturday evening.

Valdimar and Ylfa went over to Broadway to meet the manager, who called in the two doormen who had seen reason to intervene and throw Pétur out.

'It was really nothing unusual,' said the doorman, as he gulped a glass of milk at the bar.

'What do you mean by nothing unusual?' Ylfa asked as she looked around her.

The club looked drab and colourless now that all the lights were on and the place was brightly lit.

'I mean on that Saturday night there were close to a dozen dickheads we had to throw out,' he said and took a deep breath, so that his chest swelled under his tight singlet. 'There are always a few wankers who don't know how to behave, and that was just one of those occasions.'

He radiated self-confidence and rapped twice on the bar with his knuckles. He asked the member of staff behind the bar for a second glass of milk.

'Give us some more detail about this incident,' Ylfa said, making an effort to not let the man get on her nerves.

'How am I supposed to remember that?' he said, running the palm of his hand over his cropped scalp.

'Hey,' the slim club manager interrupted, frowning as he pushed his large, gold-framed glasses higher up his nose. 'We're here to help. Try to remember what happened.'

Ylfa looked sideways at him, and it occurred to her that some people didn't handle their anger well.

'All right, all right,' the doorman said, almost as if he was enjoying the attention. 'We were told that there was a bit of aggro at table thirty-two, over there,' he said, gesturing to a table by the wall. 'When we got there we found a girl squawking at this Pétur. He was all wound up and stuck his nose in the air when we asked him to calm down. He lashed out, so we showed him the door. End of story.'

'Do you recall what the people he was arguing with looked like?' Valdimar asked.

'Nah,' he said, accepting a brimming glass of milk from the barman.

'Come on,' the manager snapped impatiently. 'You must be able to remember something.'

'Hang on. How can you expect me to remember every

face? There are hundreds of people here every weekend. Maybe you need to pay me a bit more if you want me to pay more attention?' he snarled at the manager, who looked down at the paperwork in his hand. 'I vaguely remember the girl. She was screaming something at Pétur, said he'd been making trouble with the lad who was sitting at the table.'

He drank down the glass of milk in one long swallow.

'What did they look like?' Valdimar asked.

'Duh. The girl was slim and pretty, fair hair, I think. Long or longish. Just a standard typical pretty little thing. The lad had black hair. Might well have been a foreigner,' he said thoughtfully. 'I think she mentioned his name. It could have started with a P or a T...'

'It was Tony. She said Tony,' the second doorman said as he arrived, and apologised for being late.

39

'Hello, Tony. We meet again,' Valdimar said as he went into the drab interview room. He had got little more out of Oddur than he had already heard from the doormen at the night club. All the same, there was something about the account of what had happened at Broadway that troubled him and Valdimar hoped that Tony could give him a clearer picture of all this.

'Yes,' Tony muttered, his head hanging.

'Would you like something to drink? Water, or coffee?' Valdimar asked.

'No, thanks.'

'Fine,' he said, taking a seat facing Tony. 'We need to talk, and this has to be recorded.'

Valdimar switched on the tape machine that occupied the end of the table next to the wall and intoned the date, time and their names. Then he settled deeper into his chair before getting to work.

'Do you know why you're here, Tony?'

'Something to do with my father, I guess,' he said and looked up quickly at Valdimar.

'Yes. Among other things.' He took a notebook from his pocket and leafed through the pages. He took his time checking his notes before continuing. 'I'm curious to know a little more about what happened at Broadway on Saturday evening.'

'Broadway? Why?'

THE DANCER

'Tony. Let's not play games. Tell me what happened,' he said, putting a suitable amount of determination into his voice. 'And you can look at me when I'm speaking to you. I understand that an incident took place. Tell me about it.'

Valdimar allowed the silence to hang in the air and watched as Tony looked down at his hands. He couldn't let it be too short, nor could it go on for too long. It could trigger desperation and insecurity. This gave potential criminals an opportunity to put together a story, but they rarely realised just how difficult it could be to stick to it.

'You're not going to sit there in silence, are you?' Valdimar said, leaning a little closer to Tony.

'No,' he said, looking up. 'I don't get this. I went to Broadway to meet my friends.'

'Who are they, these friends of yours?'

'That's Hulda, Oddur ... and Davíð. They were there as well. Or rather, they were already there when I got there, and I didn't see them right away, so I sat at one of the tables.'

'And then?' Valdimar asked when he felt that the silence had lasted long enough.

'Then Pétur showed up and started behaving badly.'

'In what way?'

'He said things that were out of place.'

'Do you know each other?'

'No. Not at all,' he said, and paused for thought. 'We were both at the Landakot school, and I hadn't seen him since. But his behaviour didn't exactly take me by surprise. He was always pretty unpleasant at school. And he was violent.'

'What did he say to you at Broadway?'

'All sorts of things. Mostly to do with the colour of my skin. But that never bothered me. I had learned early on to ignore it, because if I, or anyone else who was on the receiving end of his bullying, responded to him, then we were giving him what he was looking for. He felt that it gave him licence to attack me, and others.'

'And did you respond to him there at Broadway?'

'No. Not to what he said. But it was annoying when he spilled his drink on me twice. That was all. But I don't get this. What am I doing here?'

'Well, I imagine you've read in the papers about the murder on Úlfarsfell?'

'Yes. Well, I heard about it on the radio. Was that Pétur?'

'Why do you think that?'

'Isn't it obvious?'

'When did you leave the nightclub?' Valdimar asked, ignoring Tony's question.

'It goes without saying that it's dreadful if he's been murdered, but what does that have to do with me? Pétur was thrown out of the club and that's the last I saw of him.'

'What time was it when you left Broadway?' Valdimar repeated.

'It must have been a little after two. Maybe close to two-thirty,' he said after a moment's thought.

'Where did you go after that?' 'I just went home.'

'Alone?'

'Yes.'

'Did you go with your friends?'

'No. I left early because my trousers were soaked after Pétur spilled his drink over me.'

'Presumably we can track down the taxi driver to confirm that.'

'Actually, no,' Tony said with a sigh as he thought things over. 'I thumbed a lift.'

'You hitched? Can you describe who picked you up, and the vehicle?'

'It was a young couple. Probably a bit younger than me. The guy had short brown hair. The girl had brownish hair as well, but long. They stopped for me when I was walking along Reykjanesbraut.'

'Fair enough,' Valdimar said, taking care not to let his

annoyance show. That description could apply to half of the country's population. 'And the car? What type of car?'

'I really couldn't tell you. It was black or dark blue. Mazda or Toyota. I'm not sure.'

'What make do you think?'

'I've no idea. I've never owned a car and don't have much interest in them.'

'Do you have the use of a car? Does your mother have a car?'

'No. I mean, I don't have the use of a car and Mum doesn't have one.'

'I see,' Valdimar said, barely able to conceal his disappointment. 'How is your mother?'

'She's in a pretty bad way.'

'Could she confirm when you came home that night?'

'Sorry. She was fast asleep. She sleeps most of the time.'

'Tell me about Sunday. When you woke up, what you did, and so on. Take me through your day,' Valdimar said with a pleasant smile.

'I was really tired when I got home and slept until almost two. I went and did some shopping around three o'clock. After that... What did I do? Yes, around five I practised dancing...'

'Where?'

'At home. I make space in the living room and often practise there.'

'All right. Go on.'

'Well, I normally practise for an hour and a half or two hours at a time. After that I went out.'

'Where to?'

'Mum wanted fish cakes for dinner. As I don't like them, I decided to go to Hornið and had something to eat there. I was there at around seven.'

'Alone?'

'Yes.' He put a hand in the inside pocket of his jacket, took out a receipt, glanced at it and slid it across the table to Valdimar. 'I paid 77 Krónur for a pizza and a coke. You can ask the waiter. He's sure to remember me because I dropped my necklace and went back the next day to see if it was there. The waiter found it.'

'I see you're not wearing it now,' Valdimar observed.

'What?' Tony said, his hand going to his throat. 'No... The clasp isn't great. That's why it keeps coming loose.'

'How long were you there, at Hornið?'

'I suppose I must have been there a couple of hours, maybe a bit less.'

'Fine. What did you do after that?'

'After that I went home and read a book until I fell asleep.' 'And can your mother confirm that?'

'She was asleep when I got home. I took the plate that was at her bedside, washed it up and then I went to bed.'

'To read?'

'Yes.'

'What's the book?'

'*Save the Last Dance for Me* by Judy Miller. It's a book about ballet.'

'Where do you work, Tony?'

'I'm unemployed.'

'So... What do you do? What do you live on?'

'My mother gets monthly payments from the state ... and from my father.'

'That no longer come through, do they?'

'No. They don't. I'm looking for work.'

'Where was the last place you worked?'

'I just haven't worked. I started at technical college but gave up after Mum was taken ill. She needs a lot of help, with the house and stuff.'

'Just so. What did you start learning at technical college?'

'Carpentry,' he said, and Valdimar noticed that he swallowed.

'What sort of maintenance needs to be done to the house?'

'Whatever needs doing. Pretty much everything. The house needs cleaning and things that go wrong need fixing. Painting, sorting out the decking in the summer, pottering with this and that.'

'Any woodwork?' Valdimar asked, his mind on the tarpaulin.

'Woodwork?'

'Yes, woodwork?'

'No' he said and thought for a moment. 'Nothing like that.'

'I ask because of what you learned at technical college.'

'No. Nothing of that nature,' Tony said and smiled.

'When did you say you last saw your father?'

'I don't remember precisely, but it could be around four years ago.'

'Don't you think it's strange that he didn't call in and see you when he was here in the summer?'

'No, not really. We weren't in touch. Like I told you, Mum and I had no idea that he was here last summer.'

40

Tony opened the heavy police station doors, and revelled in taking a breath of the cold, still outdoor air.

'What's this shit you've got us tangled up in?' demanded Davíð, from where he stood with Hulda and Oddur on the pavement.

'What do you mean?' asked Tony, who had only now noticed them and went over.

'What do I mean? Go for a night out and the next thing you know you're being interrogated at the police station. All of us separated into little boxes and given the third degree,' he said, dropping a heavy hand on his shoulder.

'Take it easy, Davíð,' Hulda said. 'So what did they ask you about?' she said, calmly addressing Tony.

'Just, y'know. What happened at Broadway. And you?' he asked, looking at them each in turn.

'Well, the same, of course,' Davíð snapped back. 'What the fuck is going on, Tony? Did you have anything to do with this Pétur?'

'Calm down,' Oddur said. 'Of course he didn't. What's got into you?'

'What's got into me? Do you know anything about Tony?' he barked, dropping his voice as two police officers made their way past and through the station doors. 'I don't. We fall in with this creep and two minutes later we're here,' he said, his voice rising back to its former volume.

'Oh, Davíð, take it easy,' Hulda said, reaching for his hand.

'None of that *Oh, Davíð* shit here,' he retorted, swatting her hand away. 'He doesn't know you at all, Hulda, but on top of everything else he reckons he loves you. You fucking...' he snarled, reaching out for Tony, who managed to side-step out of reach.

Oddur stepped smartly forward and held onto Davíð, who struggled and managed to reach out and land a resounding smack on Tony's cheek.

Tony felt the heat and the sting in his face.

You shouldn't have done that, Davíð, he thought to himself. 'Hey, we all need to calm down,' Oddur said. 'It's perfectly reasonable that the cops want to talk to us, considering what happened. We're all here, aren't we? It's not as if anyone has been arrested,' he said, putting a hand on Davíð's shoulder, which he quickly shook off.

'But what were they asking about your father, Tony?' Hulda asked, her tone mild as she caught his eye.

'Dad? I told you,' he said, and fell silent. He was still getting used to the idea that the date at Hornið had been nothing more than a mirage. He had in fact never told her anything about his father losing his life when he had been a boy.

'I don't know. Were they asking about him?'

'Just if we knew anything...'

'If we knew anything about the murder and...'

'And what?' Tony asked.

'Did you know anything about it?'

'Of course not. I didn't even know he was in the country. He left me and Mum soon after I was born and went back to the States. He was never in touch with us, and we thought he had lost his life in that crash on the ice cap.'

'I'm so sorry to hear it,' Hulda said. 'It must have been tough, all the same.'

'Jeez,' Davíð said, rolling his eyes. 'I'm out of here.'

'Sorry. See you,' Hulda said and set off after Davíð towards Hlemmur.

Tony and Oddur stood in silence and watched them go. 'So, what's happening? You busy?'

'No,' Tony said after a long pause.

'Aren't you hungry? It's getting on for nine and I've missed dinner at my Mum's place.'

'Have anything in mind?'

'There's spag bol at home, if you fancy it.'

41

The chill filled the narrow hallway when Tony and Oddur had gone through the gate and then the outside door of the two-storey house on Grundarstígur.

'It's always freezing here,' Oddur said as he shut the door behind him. 'The windows are being replaced.' He pointed at a window wrapped in plastic that leaned against the hallway wall. The wrapping was starting to come adrift. 'There are new owners here now,' he said and nodded towards the door of the downstairs flat. 'They're doing the whole place up. God knows when they'll be finished or when they'll move in. It's been like this all winter, and I haven't seen them yet.'

He gestured for Tony to follow him up the narrow, carpeted staircase leading to his attic flat. He took hold of the door handle and lifted as he pulled so that it would open.

'Isn't there a key?' Tony asked.

'Everything's falling apart here and the lock's broken. I must have called the locksmith a hundred times,' he said, throwing his jacket over the back of a chair in the kitchen. 'They must be the busiest people in the country.'

'You live here alone?'

'Yes.'

Oddur searched through a cupboard, took out a saucepan and laid the table while Tony looked round the colourful flat. The walls were painted purple, except for one that was a pale green. There were brightly coloured sheets in the doorways, tied back to hold them slightly open. There were erotic prints on the walls, and he cast an eye over a rather thin record collection in a rack next to a portable record player. Shelves on one wall were filled with jewellery cases of all shapes and sizes. These all stood open, and each one held a delicate figurine of a ballerina.

'I know, I know,' Oddur said, and laughed when he noticed Tony examining them, going closer and taking one of the cases carefully from the shelf. 'I know it sounds a bit kinky, but I collect these. For example, this one is very valuable. It's all in gold and genuine pearls. The ballerina is porcelain, and her dress is made from silk.' His voice sounded as fragile as the ballerina. 'I was on a dance tour in Russia and a friend gave me that one.'

'A boyfriend?' Tony asked, without looking at him.

'No. But he really fancied me!'

He turned a key and handed the figure in its box to Tony, and he watched the ballerina turn slow circles to the tinkling of clear but remarkably soft notes.

Oddur stood close to Tony, and he could feel the heat of his breath against his ear. He started as Oddur gently touched his back, and a rush of heat flowed through him.

Tony gently replaced the musical box on the shelf and stood motionless. The fine hairs on the back of his neck stood on end as the fingertips of Oddur's left hand touched the nape of his neck, sliding up into his hair, upwards to the back of his head. Oddur's right hand slid hesitatingly across his belly under his shirt. His fingers stroked his bare skin, slipped inside his waistband and his underwear, until they found his penis.

Oddur held Tony's hair in a grip that was gentle but firm as he drew his head back. Tony turned his head to him, and their lips touched.

Fragments of dark thoughts smashed against Tony's consciousness like storm-driven waves. As he saw the faces of his mother, his father and Pétur appear one after another, he tried to force them aside.

Tony turned to Oddur, pulled his shirt off with quick movements, and bent his head to kiss his chest and nipples. Once they had removed every stitch of each other's clothing, Tony gripped Oddur's arm tightly as he pushed him ahead and into the bedroom, where he pushed him away hard, so that Oddur landed on his back on the mattress.

He roughly took hold of him, turning him onto his front, lay on top, and eased himself inside Oddur. His left hand against the wall for support, he hooked his right arm around Oddur's neck and tightened his grip.

Tony put his face close to Oddur's and looked into his wide-open, fear-filled eyes. His hips jerked rhythmically, until his back arched as he came with a stifled animal cry.

Drained, he lay on top of Oddur, who lay motionless. For a while, Tony lay with his eyes closed, before he opened the to see that Oddur's eyes were also shut tight. His mouth was slightly open, and his face looked as if it were paralysed.

'Are you asleep?' Tony whispered.

Oddur slowly opened his eyes. He gazed at Tony.

'Am I in heaven?' he whispered.

'I don't know. Maybe.'

'That's easily the absolute best shag I've had in my whole life,' Oddur said, smiling.

42

Wednesday 8th December 1982

'Shall I throw this away? It must be completely stale by now,' Ylfa said, taking a seat in front of Valdimar's desk, where there was still one remaining slice of her sand cake. She wondered if she had overstepped a line, but Valdimar didn't seem to mind.

He stood at the window and gazed at Mount Esja across the bay. It was almost ten in the morning, but only an indistinct outline of the mountain could be made out.

'Yes, that's probably best,' he said as he took a seat. He cocked an eye towards the remnants of the cake before turning instead to the interview documents he had been reading through. 'It looks to me that all their accounts tie up, for the most part, at any rate.'

'Agreed. Hulda came across as very open. Davíð was the same, although he was very agitated.'

'What do you mean by that?' he asked, opening the top drawer of his desk.

'He was practically offended that he had been brought here. Tony certainly isn't flavour of the month with him. He said there had been a weird incident outside the National Theatre, when he declared that he loved Hulda, even though he barely knows her at all.'

'Is that so?' Valdimar muttered, opening a bottle and swallowing a tablet.

'Don't you need some water with that?' Ylfa asked when it seemed that he was struggling to get the pill down.

'Nope. It's all right,' he said, jerking his head back.

'I'll get you some water,' she said, making to stand up.

'It's all right. It's gone now.'

'What do you need to take?'

'Just some heart stuff,' he said and smiled. 'But yes. I'm curious about this Tony. To begin with, it's very strange that he should be linked to these two cases. Secondly, it all seems to add up too easily.' He leaned back in his chair and stared at the ceiling. 'It's all somehow ... too neat.'

'How so?'

'All right, he leaves Broadway before the others. He hitches a ride home. His description of the couple he says picked him up is so vague as to be useless. The couple's car is among the most common makes in the country. His mother is asleep when he gets home. I mean, this is information that's impossible to work with. The whole thing is like this.'

'We could go and have another chat with his mother.'

'Well, we could. But I don't have the feeling there's much to be gained there. We saw that before. The woman's very ill and not right in the head.'

'And what did you make of Oddur when you spoke to him?' Ylfa asked.

'He comes across as a lively enough youngster,' he said and laughed. 'You wouldn't imagine there's a bad bone in that boy's body, but you never can tell. An innocent face and manner tell you nothing about what's going on inside the man's head. But he spoke well of Tony, saying he's pleasant and good company. But he also said he's a little strange and something of a loner. But he spoke well of him.'

'Doesn't he just like him? He's quite a looker.'

'Who?'

'Tony. I mean, he's a very good-looking guy.'

'Yes, yes. But why should Oddur like him so much?'

'Come on, Valdimar.'

'He's not...?'

'Yes, he is. He tried to not make it obvious, but I saw through him. But apart from that, I got hold of the tenant on Ármúli who owed John a year's rent. He tried to be awkward, but he'll be brought in here later. I also got hold of the individual out east who was in a dispute with John over boundaries. We'll probably have to go there. It's a question of when.'

'Good,' Valdimar said, and stretched. 'It'll be interesting to hear what they have to say. Are you sure it's stale?'

'What is?'

'The cake.'

43

It was around nine when Tony woke up and saw the empty pillow next to him.

He sat up and listened for any sounds.

The place was completely silent.

He stared at the note that had been left on his neatly folded clothes on the living room table.

Hæ

Had to go and didn't want to wake you.

Are you always this beautiful in your sleep? (Stupid question)

See you soon.

Ps. Do you have a bit of a crush on me? Is this OK?

Tony smiled at the sight of the red heart Oddur had drawn after the last word.

He saw a phone and dialled the number of his grandfather's workshop.

'Hello, Grandad,' he said quietly.

'Hello, Tony. How are things? I was starting to worry about what had become of you. We need to finish this coffee table, because it's being collected today.'

'Yes, I know. I'm just feeling ill,' he said.

'What's that you said?' Jón asked, and Tony realised that he was whispering a little too quietly.

'I'm not well. I'm sorry. Can we put the coffee table off?'

'No, it's all right. I'll be able to get it done. I only need to sand down the legs and polish it. Don't worry. The next job won't be until next week, so you can just come in when you're feeling chipper. Take your time.'

'Thanks, Grandad,' Tony said. He dressed and left Oddur's flat.

44

Tony stood outside his mother's house, his eye on the open window and the curtains that hung still on this windless day.

He sensed the darkness and the silence beyond them that sapped his nerve to go inside. Neither did he have any desire to go to the ramshackle shed on Grettisgata.

After standing for a while in indecision, he decided to instead go to the National Theatre and practise for the performance. He stopped off at Vísir, picked up a Prins Polo and a bottle of Malt Extrakt, and hurried to the theatre. There was a deep silence as he went into the main entrance.

By now he was starting to get his bearings and was soon on the carpeted steps leading to the training room on the upper floor. He heard a loud grinding sound coming in through the open window as he went into the empty room. Begga took him by surprise when she appeared from her office in the far corner.

'Hello Tony, could you...?' She asked, raising her voice over the roar from outside, as she stood in the doorway, apparently struggling to keep hold of a stack of papers that she was about to drop.

Tony came to her aid, snatching hold of the pile of paper before it fell to the floor.

'Thank you. That was just in the nick of time. I couldn't find a bag,' she said and laughed. 'This endless noise is driving me mad. There's some work going on in the car park outside. But what brings you here?'

'I was just going to go through my routine,' he said with a smile.

'Excellent, excellent.' She had managed to stow the bundle of paperwork under one arm and was fussing as she tried to get the key into the lock of her office door. 'Listen, I met Davíð this morning. He told me about the interrogation. Is everything in order?'

'Yes, fine. They just wanted to talk to us about an incident at the weekend.'

'And that was to do with the young man who was found murdered?' she said as she managed to get the key to turn in the lock. 'Quite dreadful.'

'Sure. But there's nothing... I mean, it's nothing that concerns us. They just wanted some background information,' Tony said.

'But from what Davíð said, there was an altercation between the two of you. Something after a practice and again because of the interrogation.' She paused for a moment as the grinding noise outside rose to a roar. 'He's rather upset, and he wasn't exactly complimentary about you, to be completely truthful,' she added when the sound of the jackhammer outside came to an end.

'Yes, I know,' he sighed. 'It's all very unfortunate, but it'll be fine.'

'I hope so. You can't settle your differences?'

'Settle everything? Yes, that shouldn't be a problem. I like Davíð. I don't quite know what has got into him, because I know I haven't done anything to deserve this.'

'Something to do with Hulda?' she asked, clearly doubtful.

'No,' he said, looking at the floor. 'Nothing like that.'

'Well, that's good. I can't be doing with any squabbles and unexpected dramas, Tony. The performance is almost upon us, and we all have to pull together to make it a triumph. Isn't that so?'

'Absolutely. It won't be a problem.'

'That's good to hear. And I hope for your sake that they've stopped drilling. It's not the best sound to practice to,' she said and nodded towards the window. 'It's a shame I have a meeting to go to in town, otherwise I'd be with you.'

She placed the key on top of the pile of papers and took it in both hands. Just as she was about to leave the room, the noise outside started up again.

'Ach, it was too good to be true,' she said as she turned and looked at Tony with a sorrowful look in her eyes. She didn't seem to notice when the key dropped from the stack of papers to the floor.

Tony was about to take a step forward and pick up the key, but held back. He smiled at Begga.

'Hope it goes well,' she said as she shut the door behind her. Tony stood still. For a long time he looked at the door.

Then he looked at the key.

45

Tony slowly turned the key in the lock, opened the door to Begga's tiny cubbyhole of an office and fumbled for the light switch. There was none to be found, and he saw there was no light in the ceiling.

He had half-expected her to appear once she realised the key was missing.

Tony decided to bide his time, standing at the window and watching the workmen battering the tarmac of the National Theatre's car park with a jackhammer. He saw Begga march across to a burgundy Daihatsu Charade. She opened the rear door, placed the pile of papers on the seat, got behind the wheel and drove away.

He went stealthily to the door, looked around and sat down on a threadbare chair in front of the desk, and opened one of the drawers. He clicked on the desk light and adjusted it so that its yellow beam shone on the drawer's contents. Tony rapidly went through the papers that were at the top, and then spied a small key when he was about to replace them.

He glanced around and his gaze stopped at a metal filing cabinet with four locked drawers. The lock was in the top corner. He breathed more easily as the key turned in the lock.

There was nothing of any interest in the first two drawers. He opened the third, which was divided into sections containing a variety of documents. He scanned the labels and stopped at one of them, marked *scripts*. He took out a buff envelope, sat down at the desk and opened it to start reading. His heart lurched as he saw the cover.

The Dragon

A performance choreographed by Birgitte Stefánsson, 1965

A line had been put through the year and 1963 had been written underneath.

He took script from its folder, leafed quickly through it and saw that it had been widely annotated, with handwritten remarks and corrections, both between the lines of text and in the margins.

Tony was about to replace the script in its folder when he noticed a brown envelope underneath it. He extracted the contents, placed it on the table and looked at the original version of his mother's script.

'This isn't possible,' he whispered as he looked through the script. 'No. No, no.'

The yellowing paper was creased and ragged at the edges. *The Dancer* had been crossed out and *The Dragon* written by hand under it. The same went for his mother's name. Beneath the scrawl was Begga's name, Birgitte Stefánsson. The 1965 date had been changed to 1963.

Tony peered at the hand-written red lettering at the bottom of the title page, which looked to be a comment, or an opinion. He couldn't easily make it out, as the text had been crossed out. Holding it to the light, he managed to read it.

This script by Gunnhildur Jónsdóttir is worth consideration with a view to putting on a performance. I recommend that the writer be invited for an interview.

'This can't be,' he whispered as he looked down at the script. 'What have I done, Mum? What did they do to us?'

Tony ripped off part of the title page, stuffed it in his pocket and put the office back to how he had found it.

On his way out he dropped the key on the floor and ran down the stairs.

He went into the theatre's empty, silent auditorium when he reached the ground floor. He made for the centre of the space and sat in the middle of a row of seats, closing his eyes and feeling the tranquillity enveloping his body.

He opened his eyes and looked at the stage. He saw himself glide across it, as if watching a slow-motion version of himself leap and pirouette, limbs extended. He saw himself lie back, arching his back until it would go no further, screaming with every ounce of energy in his body, as blood dripped from his back to patter audibly on the boards.

Jerked from his thoughts, Tony leaned forward and listened. He heard a rhythmic tapping.

Tony stood up and made his way to the stage, and towards the sound he was sure was coming from behind the curtain. He ascended the steps to the left of the stage, pulled aside the heavy curtain and looked into the backstage darkness. He stepped further in and stood still.

He could hear a rustling.

As his eyes became accustomed to the darkness, he was able to make out the extent of the space ahead of him. He took a few slow steps further in and looked up as he heard the sound of wings. He could see a pigeon fluttering high in the tower of the building and guessed that it had come in through a high window where some light came through. The pigeon finally settled on one of the wooden platforms that lay everywhere above the stage, where the lighting crew did their work during performances.

He continued and saw the painted backdrop of houses that belonged to a well-known play, standing there as if asleep backstage, waiting to be called for the next show.

As he approached the backdrop, he saw a shaft of light from a reading lamp that illuminated the area further inside.

Tony stiffened at the sight of Oddur, standing upright, hips pumping in a slow rhythm. Tony saw the red-haired boy, trousers around his ankles, bent over the table with Oddur behind him.

After standing for a moment in silence, he was about to walk away in silence when his heel grazed against something on the floor.

Oddur looked up. The look on his face was first of surprise, and then a smile appeared when he saw Tony, who was still working out what the scene in front of him meant. He couldn't understand it, while Oddur seemed delighted to see him, his hips continued to pump.

Tony's feet seemed nailed to the floor. Oddur's smile broadened, and he gestured for him to come closer. He could barely prevent himself from believing that this was yet another mirage. How could he tell? How was he supposed to tell reality from fantasy after the incident with Hulda?

Tony walked towards Oddur when he saw his beckoning finger. He could feel the pressure building inside his head until it became unbearable. He felt his head swim, stopping, and then hurrying back and down from the stage.

Once he was standing outside the National Theatre he had no idea if the evening, or anything else, could be real. His thoughts went to his mother, and he wondered if she was in bed now and calling for him.

Tony stuck a hand in his pocket and took out the creased scrap of paper he had ripped from the title page of the script. At any rate, that was real.

The same went for the rage that seethed inside him and which he was unable to shake off.

Tony walked along Öldugata, opened the door and went cautiously inside. There was a heavy smell to the place, verging on sour. He switched on the light in the hall, and then in the kitchen. The light from there threw a little brightness into the living room.

After standing in the kitchen doorway for a while,

knocking his knuckles against the door frame, which did nothing but magnify the roaring in his head, he went into the living room and stood still in front of his mother where she sat in the wheelchair, eyes wide open. He stared at her arms, drooping lifeless on each side of the wheelchair. These were the arms that had once curved into a beautiful bow, her fingers trembling like blades of grass as she danced. These were the fingers that had been applied to the typewriter keys as they stamped their letters on paper. These were the fingers that had punched in every letter of *The Dancer*.

'I'm so sorry, Mum. You must forgive me. I didn't know,' he moaned, falling to his knees and wrapping his arms about her. 'I can't take any more. From now on nobody's going to hurt us or betray us. Just you see, Mum. I'll make sure,' he said as he got to his feet and wiped away the tears.

He gazed at her for a moment, kissed her forehead and went to the kitchen where he opened a drawer and took out a carving knife.

Tony left the flat.

46

Thursday 9th December 1982

'Here, darling,' Ásta said as she handed Valdimar a glass of water and his blood pressure tablet.

'Thanks, darling. I could have fetched it for myself,' he said gently, without taking his eyes from the screen.

The reporter had a miserable look about him. Valdimar wondered if it was because this was a new face being beamed into the homes of Icelanders by state TV, or because of the nature of the news item he had been given to report on.

Most of us know the swan pair Svanur and Svandís, who have enchanted everyone as they settled in at Hljómskálagarður here in Reykjavík. But they are no longer with us. This was the shocking sight that met a young mother walking with her child this morning as she found the pair of swans lying beside the path. It seems that someone has ... I don't exactly know how to put this ... slaughtered them. As if that's not enough, their wings have been removed. We have these accompanying pictures.

'What on earth is wrong with people?' Ásta asked as she sat at his side on the sofa. 'Where's the world heading to, Valdi?'

'I simply have no idea,' Valdimar sighed.

'Shall I take your plate?' she asked. 'Valdimar?' she added firmly when there was no response.

'No, thanks,' he said with a smile, although he kept that

to himself. She only used his proper name when something irritated her, or when she needed to get his attention.

'I'll take the plate. I can see you don't want it.'

Valdimar looked at the plate. He had finished the fish and potatoes, and some of the vegetables. It had been after a consultation with the doctor that these portions of broccoli and cabbage had become a little too large, and out of proportion with the rest of the contents of his plate. He knew that he needed to watch his diet and lose a few kilos, and that Ásta meant well. He had fought plenty of battles over the years and had long ago worked out that there was no point arguing with her.

'No, it's all right. Of course I'm going to finish it,' he said, as if he were excited, as he also tried to convince himself that he was doing this for his own good – and not for her sake. All the same, it wasn't easy to make himself believe that, as he found broccoli bloody terrible. He was about to put a morsel in his mouth when the phone at his side rang.

After speaking to the person on the other end of the line, humming and grunting in agreement, he ended the conversation with 'have a good trip,' and replaced the receiver.

'Who was that?' Ásta asked.

'That was Ylfa. She's travelling to Egilsstaðir to meet the landowner.'

47

Ylfa sat on the hard bench and waited for the flight to be called. She looked at the half-eaten bun she had picked up at the cafeteria. She had no appetite, dropped it in a bin and stared out of the window. She wondered if there would even be a flight now that snow was falling again.

She saw a young couple walk towards the terminal pulling behind them a little girl who sat on a red sledge. The two of them held each other tight, and once inside the building, hugged tenderly. The woman lifted the child, held her in her arms, and then waved good-bye and the man and the little girl walked back. The young woman took off her coat, adjusted the airline brooch on her lapel, and went through the staff entrance.

Ylfa wiped away tears before they had a chance to reach her cheeks. She had stopped off at her mother-in-law's house on the way to the airport.

*

Steinthór had a sleepy look about him when he opened the door of the flat on Álfheimar.

'Hœ. Did I wake you up?' Ylfa asked, forcing a smile.

'Yeah. Fell asleep in front of the TV,' he said blandly.

'I see,' she said, and they looked at each other. Neither of them said anything. 'I just wanted to check up on you both,' she said at last. 'Is the little 'un awake?' she asked hopefully.

'No. She's asleep.'

'So,' she said, and her shoulders slumped. 'Aren't you going to ask me in? I'd love to see her ... and you, of course.'

'Ach. Dad's not well and he's dozing on the sofa. He thinks he has a temperature,' he said, haltingly, after glancing behind him into the flat. 'And dinner's on the table. Can't you come tomorrow?'

'Aren't you coming home? What's going on, Steini?' she asked, her voice doleful.

'I really don't know, Ylfa,' he said after a long pause. 'It's ... I don't know if ... Uh, can't we talk about this tomorrow?'

'Steini, I know I've been working a lot ... Everyone has to work and make a few sacrifices...'

'Yeah, that's just it,' he interrupted. 'We all need to make sacrifices, but this has to work both ways, Ylfa. Your sacrifices only go one way, and that's work.'

'I...'

'Ach. Please, Ylfa. Come tomorrow. Or the next day, or the day after that,' he said, gradually inching the door shut.

Ylfa wasn't sure how long she stood looking at the door before she turned and left.

*

Ylfa got to her feet as the flight was announced and walked out to the aircraft.

She thought of her daughter as she climbed the boarding steps and wondered whether or not it was time to resign from the police.

THE DANCER

48

Mick Jagger's voice boomed from the cassette player's speakers. An empty black plastic sack lay on the floor by the lathe. Rivulets of blood trickled from it and along the floor.

Tony stood bare-chested at the lathe. His torso and hands were speckled with blood, and white feathers. He lifted up what he had made and smiled at the sight of the white wings. He had fixed them in pairs, making the spread of the wings even more impressive, sewing them with strong twine to a white leather jacket. The jacket had been one of his mother's favourites back when her need to party had been at its height. Tony had cut off the arms, and now he put on the jacket. He went over to the mirror and turned this way and that as he dispassionately examined his own reflection. The wings drooped a little behind him, but lifted as he zipped up the jacket and the leather tightened about his torso.

Tony fetched a wooden cigar box, opened it, and counted the ten thimbles inside. Tony picked them up one by one, pressing them onto his fingertips. He inspected the swan claws he had carefully fixed to the end of each thimble.

He stood as if mesmerised in front of the mirror. His face impassive, he raised his left hand to his chest, pressed the claws to his skin and drew his hand diagonally down, slowly. Five red wheals formed on his skin, the wounds bleeding in a few places. He stared for a while at his own reflection before taking off the jacket and placing it carefully on the table. When he had counted the thimbles back into the cigar box, he fetched a stool and used it to reach for an orange bag containing a tent from its place on the rafters. Tony took the tent out, and instead placed his creation in the bag, along with the box of thimbles.

He went over to the lathe and spun the wheel to release the wooden club he had made. Once he had cleaned up any sign that he had been in the workshop, he switched off the cassette player and turned off the lights.

Then he left the workshop.

49

Tony parked in front of the house where Davíð lived on Ásvallagata. He gazed along the deserted street and the sight of the yellow cones of brightness that illuminated the street below each street light was somehow comforting.

It was a windless night, but bitterly cold. Startled as the ice beneath his feet cracked while he made his way stealthily through the garden, Tony was concerned that he might have attracted attention. He took care to keep to the edges of the garden and to stay away from the light that flooded out from the living room window.

Tony approached the back of the house from where light came from an open window at ground level. Grey vapour rose through the opening and disappeared into the darkness.

When Tony came closer and peered through the gap in the curtains, he caught sight of Davíð in the shower cubicle, where he had not bothered to draw the shower curtain across.

Tony stood with his back to the wall as Davíð turned off the water, whistling a few notes of a familiar tune.

A moment later muted light came from the living room window. Tony worked his way closer and looked inside. Davíð stepped across the living room with a towel around his waist and switched the television on. After browsing a couple of tapes, he selected one and put it into the player. Davíð let the towel drop to the floor before stretching out on the sofa, arranging pillows and pulling a duvet up to his middle.

The movie started and Davíð turned up the volume.

Tony approached the bathroom window. He could hear sounds from inside, gunshots, shouts and cries.

He gingerly reached inside and lifted the bar holding the window in place from the jamb. He drew the canvas tent bag towards him, lifted the window fully open and stretched inside to let the bag slide to the bathroom floor. He took a sharp breath as the bag sagged and fell to one side, landing against the toilet seat with an audible click.

As quickly as he could, Tony edged along to the living room window, and saw that Davíð hadn't noticed anything. He went back to the bathroom window, held it open with his right hand, and eased himself inside, feet first.

Tony stood completely motionless as he listened. He could feel the moisture in the air against his skin. The light blue tiles were damp and the mirror over the bathroom sink was still misted. He carefully took hold of the door, biting his lip as he eased it shut.

He opened the bag, took hold of the wings in both hands and lifted up his creation. Tony removed all his clothes, then slipped on the winged leather jacket and placed a thimble on each finger. Then he took the club from the bag.

Tony went to the door and took hold of the wooden handle. He looked down at his hand and hesitated. He let go.

He drew several deep breaths and looked down at his whitened knuckles as he again took hold of the handle and pushed it down.

Tony snorted and was about to open the door when he heard a warm voice. This was different from the tones coming from the television. He let go of the door handle, put his ear to the door and listened.

The sound was muffled, but he could hear the

conversation more clearly once the sound from the television was muted.

'Sweetheart, did you miss me?' a woman's voice asked.

'Yes, I thought you weren't coming,' Davíð said.

'You smell so good.'

He heard their laughter and a clatter as something was upset. Then there was silence and as Tony pressed his ear to the door, he could hear his own pounding heartbeat, his chest pressed hard against the wood.

Tony slipped off the thimbles when the woman's voice carried to him.

'Wait, wait. I need to go to the toilet first.'

Tony snatched up his clothes and the bag and stepped into the shower cubicle. As he drew the shower curtain across, he dropped one of the thimbles which tinkled on the tiled floor in front of the door. The door opened and Tony heard the metal thimble scrape across the floor as it was pushed to the wall.

Tony saw the outline of Hulda's naked body through the narrow opening between the shower curtain and the wall as she went past.

He heard her pee, and a moment later the toilet flushed. After she had washed her hands she went towards the door, pausing in front of the shower cubicle. Tony held his breath and gazed at her shadowy form through the shower curtain. He could see her profile as she drew back her hair. She suddenly stooped down, and Tony thought of the thimble. She stood up, and slipped a band around her hair, pulling it back into a ponytail. He saw her outline vanish, and couldn't be sure if she was stepping away, or towards the shower cubicle. He tightened his grip on the club.

'Feel like a fuck?' she asked gaily as she opened the door and left the room.

50

Friday 10th December 1982

'I have to say, I'm extremely proud of you all,' Begga said, looking down at the dance troupe that now sat, hot and panting, on the stage. 'I couldn't be happier with the way everything flowed, that was just flawless. Your interpretation of the wolf was wonderful, Oddur. Sharp, powerful, lithe. The same goes for you, Davíð. You were so... regal, and poetic. Excellent,' she said, sending him a smile.

Tony looked at Davíð as he winked at Hulda. He thought of how narrowly Hulda had unwittingly saved his life the previous evening. After scrambling out through the bathroom window, he had peered in through the living room window and saw how Hulda straddled Davíð, sinuously rocking back and forth.

He glanced at her where she sat smiling on the stage, her eyes smouldering as she looked at Davíð.

When he looked over at Oddur, who smiled to himself as if he was still digesting Begga's praise, there was just one word that came to mind: betrayer.

'And the closing scene. When you came in, Tony. Your interpretation of the dragon was simply outstanding,' Begga said, jerking him from his own thoughts. 'I look forward to seeing you at the opening night tomorrow when you show that explosive energy that's inside you. And that'll be before a packed house. I mean, I'm fully convinced of the dragon's hatred as he squeezes the life out of the wolf, not to mention the swan. Don't you agree, kids? It was a delight to see that power, but at the same time such grace. You have a fantastic mastery of movement, Tony.'

He returned her gaze and forced a smile. He could feel his lips tremble as the anger surged inside him, as if a predator had woken from a deep sleep.

'What we need to bear in mind tomorrow is the feeling for the space and the proximity to the audience. We need to be enchanting, and seductive...'

'Can I ask something?' Tony broke in.

'What did you say?' Begga asked.

'There's something I'd like to ask,' he said, his eyes flickering over the assembled group. He already regretted having spoken up. He had the feeling that he himself hadn't been ready when the question tripped out of him.

'Yes. Of course, Tony,' she said, going over to him.

'I've read the script and the story is wonderful. All that love, and how hatred manages to... kill it,' he said, looking ahead of him as if in a dream. 'There's all that rage and no mercy for those who are trying to live and survive. I find it unbelievable that you are able to portray evil in such a way that it appears so mundane. It's as if we're supposed to embrace it. Even forgive it. It's as if that was never even discovered and...'

'And what's your question?' Begga asked gently, and Tony was aware of smothered laughter among the group.

'I wanted to ask how you got the idea for this work?'

'What kind of stupid question is that?' Davíð sneered. Tony looked up and saw Oddur holding in laughter.

'It's not a stupid question, Davíð. There's something remarkable behind it. When I was a young girl I suffered a traumatic experience... and I won't go into that here. But afterwards, I suffered from nightmares for many years,' she said and paced the stage thoughtfully. 'These were terrible nightmares. So we can say that this work was forged in that nightmare dreamworld. Yes, let's put it like that. It came to me in a dream.'

There was silence on the stage – until Begga clapped her hands three times.

'This isn't something we need to dwell on. Once again, wonderful flow, and we meet here at six tomorrow. The performance starts at eight.'

THE DANCER

51

Tony walked into the darkness of the flat on Öldugata.

The rehearsal performance had left him exhausted, and he had gone back to Grettisgata to try to sleep. That wasn't easy, as his landlady had clearly seen him arrive. She made repeated attempts to reach him, banging again and again on the door. Tony suspected what she was after, as he had noticed that her steps were once again beneath a thick covering of snow. But in between the knocks on the door, he was unable to rest with his head on the filthy mattress. Dark images made constant assaults on his thoughts – especially after he had left the National Theatre and saw Oddur joyfully greeting the red-haired boy Tony had seen him with backstage.

It was getting dark and when it was obvious that his restlessness wasn't going to give him any peace to sleep, he slipped out and hurried home to Öldugata.

'Hi there, Mum,' he said, after standing for a long time in the kitchen doorway, summoning the courage to go into the living room.

He put a record on the record player, poured her a drink that he put on the table beside her and sat in front of the wheelchair.

'Mother, could we just pretend that you're alive? Can we do that?' he said, touching her cold hand.

'Is that so?' he said after sitting in silence, looking at her, listening.

'Thanks, Mum. Of course I'll do that.'

He reached for the glass, mimed giving her a drink from it, and took a big gulp himself.

He coughed and retched as he looked into the glass. He held it again to his lips as he threw his head back and forced himself to swallow the contents, until there wasn't a drop left in the glass. Then he hurled it across the living room so that it smashed against the watercolour on the wall.

He lay back, resting the back of his head against his mother's leg.

'I'm sorry, Mum. Yes, of course I'll clean it up. What was that? Well, that goes without saying,' he said, stood up and began to pull his clothes off.

He tried to lace up the ballet shoes, and as he was completing the final knot, he felt his body begin to tremble. The tears trickled as he swayed his body back and forth and turned in slow circles.

Tony went to the cupboard, took out a bottle and took a long drink from it.

He continued to dance.

'Sorry, Mum. I know, I know,' he said and stood still. 'I'm not doing well. I'm never going to get it right, am I? I can't dance,' he slurred between sobs. 'I'll never dance like you, Mum. You've always been right,' he continued.

Tony spun on the spot, lost his balance and crashed against the wall.

'I miss you, mother!' he yelled, as he flung the bottle that hit the curtains and broke the living room window.

He went over to the window. The bottle had smashed through the single pane of glass. He was about to draw the curtain again when he saw the neighbour's black Labrador sniffing in the garden below the window.

Tony went back over to his mother, collapsed on the floor before the wheelchair and laid his head in her lap.

'It'll soon be over, Mum. I promise,' he murmured.

THE DANCER

He was about to fall asleep when he jerked into wakefulness and sat up. He stood up, marched to the kitchen, opened the fridge and took out the saucepan containing the remains of the stew. He went quickly to the door.

52

'Good morning,' Ylfa said from the doorway, after knocking gently and opening the door of Valdimar's office.

'Morning, there you are,' he said as he took off his glasses and put down the documents he had been reading. 'How did it go in Egilsstaðir?'

'There wasn't a lot that came out of it,' she said, taking a seat. 'The man had certainly been at loggerheads with John. They have adjoining parcels of land and there have been legal squabbles going on for years over where the boundaries lie. But he has an alibi that I was able to confirm.'

'Fair enough,' Valdimar said. 'We can cross him off the list, at any rate. The same goes for the tenant on Ármúli. We had a chat, and he owes John a heap of money in unpaid rent, but he has a solid alibi.'

'So are we back to square one, or what?'

'I don't know. I've been going over these papers relating to Tony,' he said, gesturing at the documents on the desk in front of him. 'There's something about him that bugs me, and it won't leave me alone.' He tapped his forehead with his index finger. 'But can I ask you something, Ylfa?' he ventured, and leaned forward over the desk.

'Yes, of course,' she replied, after a moment's silence.

'It seems to me that you're a little down. Is there something bothering you, or...' he fell silent as her gaze dropped to the floor. 'We don't need to talk about this if it's uncomfortable for you.'

'A few problems at home,' Ylfa said, looking up at him. 'Nothing that can't be fixed ... I hope.' Her eyes went to the window. 'We have a little daughter, and I haven't been...'

'There's a visitor for you,' said a police officer who made a sudden appearance in the doorway.

'A visitor?' Valdimar said, glancing at the clock to see that it was almost six. 'Who is it?'

'The farmer from Úlfarsfell. He says he's called a few times in connection with information about Pétur's murder.'

'Yes, and?' Valdimar said. 'Why hasn't this information reached us?'

'Well, I'm not sure about that ... he's on the eccentric side.'

'Meaning what?'

'I get the feeling he's a few sandwiches short of a picnic.'

'Sandwiches? Picnics? What are you talking about?'

'He means that he's not sure that the man's all there, Valdimar,' Ylfa said gently and smiled at the officer. 'We'll be right with you.'

They went down to reception to find a bony elderly man in a shabby blue Álafoss coat sitting hunched in a chair at one of the tables. The reception area was otherwise deserted, and they sat down next to him.

'I've tried to call a good few times,' the man said in a voice so loud that Valdimar and Ylfa exchanged glances.

'That's unfortunate...' Ylfa said.

'What was that?' the man asked, leaning closer to her.

'I said, that's unfortunate,' she replied, raising her voice.

'Officers went twice to your home to talk to you about this. But both times there was nobody home.'

'That's impossible,' he said, and sounded as if he were upset. 'I'm always at home.'

'So tell me,' Valdimar said, his voice raised to a level that Ylfa felt was taking things too far. 'What is it you want to tell us?'

'Well, I saw the car,' he said, switching his gaze to Valdimar.

'What car?'

'The one that drove up the hill that night when the murder took place.'

'What?'

Ylfa was about to say the same but stopped herself. She noticed the officer behind the reception desk trying to hide a smirk.

'And what kind of vehicle was this?'

'A van. I was tinkering with the generator in the shed by the road that runs up the hill when he drove past.'

'Do you have a clear description?' Valdimar asked.

'That I do. It was yellowish or light brown. And there was something trailing behind it.'

'Really? And what was that?'

'I don't know about that. My guess is it was the exhaust pipe. It was that kind of rattling noise.'

'Did you see the driver?' Valdimar asked.

'No.'

'And when was this?' Ylfa asked.

'It was a quarter past twelve. I saw it clearly. Just for a change, it wasn't snowing, and the weather was as fine as it gets. All the same, the forecast doesn't look good...'

'Did you see the van return?'

'Yes,' he said firmly. 'I was standing at the kitchen window when he came down the hill about two hours later. And that was the only vehicle to go up the track that night.'

'You didn't see the licence plate, did you?' Valdimar asked, not expecting to get a positive response.

'No, I didn't see that. But I saw what was on the side of the van, even though it was pretty faded.'

'A logo?' Ylfa asked, sitting up straighter.

'That's it, a logo. I'd just started the generator when the van went past. There's a light by the egg sign...'

'The egg sign?' Valdimar said.

'Yes, I sell eggs. The generator keeps me supplied with electricity, including lighting up the sign. I clearly saw the company symbol on the side of the van when it went past. But I didn't manage to read the lettering. Maybe it was dirty. But hold on,' he said, and felt in his pocket. 'When I heard what had happened up on the hill, I put two and two together. I was sure that this would interest you.' He fumbled with difficulty with his coat pocket. 'That's why I've been trying to get through to you for days.' He finally extracted a creased scrap of paper and pushed it across to them. 'I scribbled that down, the van and the symbol.'

*

Once the man had gone, Valdimar sat at his desk and called the editor of *Morgunblaðið*, who picked up immediately. They had been on good terms through the years and had become good friends. After assuring each other that their families were in fine health, Valdimar got to the point.

'There's a picture that needs to go into tomorrow's paper.'

'You're asking a lot, Valdi. The presses should be rolling already.'

'Then you'll have to stop them. Do it right away, will you? And let me know,' Valdimar said, and ended the call.

The picture and a few lines of text had barely gone through the fax machine when the phone rang.

'You're a lucky dog, Valdi,' the editor said. 'Something held the presses up, so we can get this in. It'll be in tomorrow morning's paper.'

53

Tony's hips swayed slightly to the beat of the music as he stood bare-chested in front of the mirror in the workshop. He ran his fingertips over the red scratches on his chest. His torso was covered in dark bloodstains.

He stepped closer to the mirror and adjusted the bloody teeth he had put in his mouth. After trying to get them to stay in place, he took them out and went over to the workbench. He fixed the dog's jaws in the vice and cut deeper grooves into the bone with a small grinder so that there would be space for his own teeth. He loosened the vice, looked the jaws over carefully and checked the bite as he moved them up and down.

Tony replaced it in his mouth and reached for the cigar box. He took out one of the thimbles on which he had replaced the swan claws with the sharper claws he had extracted from the Labrador, and which he had sharpened even more.

Standing before the mirror, he growled, long and deep.

Tony looked at the clock, which showed it was almost two in the morning.

'You're no pussy cat. You're a wolf,' he muttered as he bundled the remains of the dog into a black bag. 'Shall I bite your throat? Shall I bite your throat?' he continued, his voice shrill.

He dipped a mop in water and washed away the blood from below the workbench.

'Your interpretation of the wolf was wonderful, Oddur. Sharp, powerful...' he thought for a moment. 'Yes, and lithe,' he said, mimicking and theatrically exaggerating Begga's tone as he put the thimble and the jaws into a small toolbox.

He switched off the tape player, went to the door and glanced back over the workshop.

He turned out the light.

'Shall I bite your throat? Shall I bite your throat?' he demanded, sending his deep, hoarse voice into the darkness.

54

Tony pulled the glass and the plastic apart, crawled through the window in the porch and went up the stairs to Oddur's attic flat in the house on Grundarstígur. He stood still and listened, cautiously put a hand on the door handle and squeezed it downwards. He heard the lock click as he lifted the door a little to ease it open. He closed the door carefully behind him.

There was complete silence in the carpeted flat and the only ray of brightness came from the street lamp below the kitchen window.

Tony went to the bedroom, put down the toolbox and the club, and spied where Oddur lay in the bed, the duvet bunched between his legs, and his back to him.

He picked up the figurine Oddur had shown him and looked at himself in the tiny mirror inside the lid, before putting it down again. He took hold of the little handle on the back and turned it a few times so that a couple of faint clicks came from inside the case. Then he put it back on the shelf. Then he undressed, put the jaws in his mouth and pushed the thimbles onto the tips of his fingers.

On his way to the dark bedroom, he picked up the figurine and put it carefully on the little round table beside the bed. He stood at the end of the bed, listening to Oddur's steady breathing.

Oddur whimpered as Tony opened the figurine's box and its piercing tones echoed around the room as the statuesque ballerina with her arms raised high began to slowly twirl.

'What's that?' he said hoarsely, lifting himself up onto one elbow. 'What's going on? Tony, is that you?' he called, flinching and blinking rapidly as he looked up to where Tony stood with the club held in both hands above his head.

55

Saturday 11th December 1982

It was getting dark, and the wind ruffled the curtains by the broken window in the living room.

Tony woke on the sofa and immediately tasted the bitter flavour of metal as he wiped drool from his lips. He turned his hands slowly back and forth as he looked at their covering of black, dried blood.

His foot connected with something on the floor as he sat up and he saw the bloody jawbone and the thimbles that lay scattered on the floor by the sofa.

He tried to recall the events of the night before and he could hear the whoosh of the club somewhere inside his head, just as it had when it had whistled through the air to smash with all the force he could summon into Oddur's skull.

*

After the blow had connected, Tony had thrown himself on him, snatched at his hair and dragged his head back. He remembered looking for a moment at his neck, before opening his mouth and sinking the dog's sharp teeth into Oddur's throat. After that were only indistinct flashes of memory in which he furiously tore and scratched at Oddur's skin with the sharp claws.

THE DANCER

He could barely catch his breath as he straddled the motionless body ... like a wolf.

*

It took a while for Tony to realise where he was, and he was startled at the sight of his mother in the wheelchair. He watched her, as if waiting for her to speak.

Tony stood up and noticed that day's *Morgunblaðið* when he went past the front door. He picked the newspaper up as he went as if in a daze to the bathroom.

He gazed for a long time at the sketch of the van before he looked up and saw his own blood-streaked face in the mirror.

56

Tony turned to walk up Klapparstígur when he saw a police car coming along Hverfisgata.

He had meant to go down to Vitastígur, certain that he had no time to lose. So despite the risk, as the description that had appeared in *Morgunblaðið* was quite accurate, he had taken the decision to take the van. The request for information mentioned two possible makes of van and possible colours. But what concerned Tony most was the logo on the side of a crossed hammer and saw. When he reached Vitastígur, he waited anxiously in the van for his grandfather to leave the workshop. He felt a lump in his throat as he watched him walk with slow, careful steps up the snow-covered pavement of Vitastígur. He wondered if his life might have turned out to be different if Jón had been able to save him when he was a child. He alone had shown Tony any love and affection.

As soon as Jón was out of sight, Tony got out of the van and went into the workshop. He picked a tape from the box and put it in the player. The strings and choir of Bach's *Hallelujah* echoed through the workshop.

He fetched the cardboard box of cutlery and tableware that Jón had inherited from his own parents. He counted out ten steak knives and in a piece of theatrical role-play, laid them out on the bench as his body swayed to the music.

He sawed the sharp point from each knife and the sparks

flew as he fixed them one by one in the vice and applied the grinder to the steel.

57

'It's almost six,' Ylfa said when Valdimar asked what time it was. They had been through all the paperwork relating to John and Pétur, and the sheer amount of information had left them exhausted.

Valdimar had spoken at length with Ævar, who told him that the tarpaulin from the crime scene on Úlfarsfell and the tarpaulin used to wrap John's body were not similar. Analysis of the stains on the tarpaulins had still not led to any concrete conclusions.

Ylfa sat silent in the chair facing Valdimar's desk as she checked through items listed on a pad. There had been dozens of calls throughout the day about the van described in *Morgunblaðið*. Not one of them had turned out to be the one they were looking for.

'He's bugging me, this Tony,' Valdimar said absently.

'What do you mean?'

'I can't quite put my finger on it. Do you believe in coincidences?'

'Yes, and no,' she replied, after a moment's consideration.

'I've always thought it's a question of the point at which coincidence meets arithmetic. For example, I'll never forget when I flew to Paris, which is a city of millions of inhabitants. I was going to meet school friends who were studying there. They sent me directions for how to get to where they lived, but I couldn't find the place and got lost. So I went – by coincidence - into a bar to take a better look at the map. Guess who was sitting there?' he said with a smile.

'Your friends?' said Ylfa, who had listened with interest.

'Precisely!' he said, slapping the desk with the flat of his hand. 'So Tony turning up in two, apparently unconnected, cases has me thinking. Coincidence, or arithmetic? Aren't those kids having their opening night tonight?'

'Yes, I think so.' She leafed through the interview notes. 'It's at eight.'

'I think I might drop in,' Valdimar said.

'What for? What do you want to ask him about?'

'Nothing. Nothing at all. I just want him to know that we're keeping an eye on him. There's something he's not telling us,' he said, standing up. 'I'd better be on my way.'

'Already? The show isn't for a while yet,' she said in surprise.

'I know. First I'm going to go and fetch my car. I took it to be fixed this morning and it's ready.'

'Now? Aren't they closed?'

'No,' he said and Ylfa heard him snort. 'It's a pal of mine and he does repairs in his garage. See you later,' he said, opening the door.

'Fine. I'll see you there. I need to go through ... a few things here before I'm finished,' she said in an undertone, as she turned around in the chair and realised that Valdimar had gone.

Ylfa stretched, looked at the phone and decided to call Steinthór. She was startled to hear a rustling sound as someone answered the phone.

'Hello? Hello?' She said, pressing the receiver tight against her ear.

'Hello,' Steinthór said after a long pause.

'Hæ. Ylfa.'

'Well, I recognise your voice,' he replied cheerfully, although Ylfa had the feeling there was a note of sarcasm behind it. 'What was all that noise?'

'The little one answered the phone. Meaning that she picked up the receiver.'

'I see,' she said, and the feeling of loss surged through her.

'Give her the phone, would you? I want to hear her voice,' she said, trying to sound happy.

'Not right now, Ylfa. Dinner's ready and we're about to sit down to eat.'

'Steini, are you shutting me out? I want to see my daughter. And I want to see you as well,' she added, aware that her voice was about to crack. 'I miss you terribly.' There was a long silence. 'Are you there?'

'Yes. I'm here,' he said, his voice gentler. 'Call in ten minutes or so. I'll feed her right away and then you can talk, gaga, googoo, and all that.'

'All right,' she said, and put the phone down.

She laughed to herself, feeling a wave of relief. She felt that time had stood still, and she decided to go back through the notes in her pad, when the phone rang.

'Ylfa,' she said.

'Evening,' said the familiar voice of one of her police colleagues. 'I was pretty sure you'd still be at work. There's someone called Jón on the line. Says he knows something about the van.'

'Put him through,' she sighed.

'What can I do for you?' she asked when she had introduced herself.

'It's about that van.'

'Yes? You think you recognise it?' she asked.

'Yes, coming!'

'What?'

'Sorry. I've been having dinner with some friends. They showed me the sketch in the paper and asked if I recognised the van. Which I do.'

'How so?'

'Because it's my van.'

'What did you say?' she asked in astonishment.

'Going by the drawing, then that's my van. Unless there are other brown Chevy vans around with that logo on the side,' he said, sounding relaxed. 'I'm wondering why you're so interested in it.'

'Do you have the vehicle at the moment?'

'No, not right now.'

'So who's driving it?'

'That's my grandson, Tony.'

'And do you know where he is now?' she asked, getting to her feet.

'No, I'm not sure. I imagine he's at home. He hasn't been well, poor lad.'

'Isn't he taking part in a dance performance tonight?'

'Dance? Tonight?'

'That's right. At the National Theatre. There's an opening night performance by the dance troupe at eight o'clock, and it's about to start,' she said, glancing at the clock.

'I've heard nothing about this. An opening night?'

58

The snow was coming down hard as Ylfa drove slowly along Öldugata, looking around in the hope of seeing the van.

After the conversation with Jón, she glanced at the clock and realised that her ten minutes were up, and it was time to call Steini back. She hesitated by the phone and finally made her decision. She knew that time was tight.

She picked up the phone and called.

'Good evening Ásta, my name's Ylfa,' she said when she had almost given up hope that anyone was going to answer. 'I'm working on an investigation with Valdimar.'

'Yes, hello. I knew about that,' Ásta said.

'Is he there?' she asked, sounding hurried.

'No,' Ásta said slowly. 'He's not home yet.'

'I see. Do you have a number for his ... friend? The mechanic?'

'Brandur? No, I'm sorry.'

After speaking to Ásta, she had the feeling that there was no time to waste getting to Öldugata.

*

She parked in the nearest empty space further down the street and walked towards the house. There were no lights to be seen.

Ylfa rang the bell several times, checked along the sides

of the house and noticed curtains flapping from one of the windows. She went closer and examined the broken glass.

The window was set too high in the wall for her to be able to look inside. Ylfa looked around until she noticed a square-shaped pile of rubbish by the fence that encircled the house. When she had brushed away the snow, a stack of planks appeared. She struggled to extract one of them, but once it was free, she placed it by the wall of the house and stood on it to give herself something to push against as she lifted herself up and caught hold of the window sill.

Ylfa moved the curtain aside to let some of the brightness of the street light shine in.

She couldn't work out right away what she found herself looking at. It took a while for her to realise that she was staring straight at Gunnhildur's pale face.

The third time she slammed her elbow against the glass of the front door, it gave way. She reached inside to unlock it.

'Hello?' Ylfa called in a low voice, a hand over her face. She went slowly into the hall and from there to the living room, switched on the light in the corner, and stood in shock as she saw Gunnhildur's drained face and the grey spume that had leaked from her mouth and nose. Ylfa felt revulsion well up inside her and she retched. She hadn't realised that she had instinctively backed away, until she became aware that there was someone standing behind her. She spun around and gasped as she looked into his face.

59

Tony had finished shaping the knife points and fixing them to the thimbles. He ran one of the blades just hard enough over the tip of his index finger and watched blood well up from the broken skin.

He checked the time and decided it was time to be on his way to the National Theatre. He cleared everything away and put the cigar box containing the thimbles into the toolbox. After looking over the workbench and rooting through the toolbox, he found that he had forgotten the jawbone.

Tony hurried along Öldugata and parked across the pavement, got out of the van and was about to walk over to the house when he hesitated. He was certain that he had switched off the living room light. He gently closed the driver's door and padded as quietly as he could to the front door, which stood slightly ajar.

Pushing the door cautiously open, Tony took care to avoid stepping on broken glass. He went with silent steps and looking into the living room, he saw the jawbone on the floor by the sofa. A chill of uncertainty rushed through him as he stood motionless, trying to figure things out.

He was about to take a step forward when he heard a sound of someone retching around the corner in the living room. He advanced carefully, until he saw Ylfa's back. He was right behind her when she turned around.

Their eyes met, each holding the other's gaze for what

seemed like an eternity, until Tony lashed out with a heavy punch to her face. Ylfa fell back but managed to kick out at Tony's leg as he approached her.

Ylfa fought to stand up, hooking an arm around Tony's neck as he tumbled over the wheelchair. He could feel his airway being choked and tried to jab his elbow into her as she hung on tight on his back. He landed two punches to Ylfa's face, and she tightened her grip.

The pressure behind his eyes was becoming unbearable and he was starting to see his surroundings through a mist. Tony powered backwards with a couple of rapid steps, so that Ylfa crashed against the window sill and lost her grip on his throat.

Tony fumbled, grabbed a heavy vase and let fly towards Ylfa's head.

His breathing came in short gasps as he supported himself, crouched with his hands on his knees, looking down at Ylfa's motionless body.

He fetched pairs of tights from his mother's bedroom and used them to tie Ylfa's hands behind her back. He hauled her to the kitchen, where he dumped her into a chair and used another pair of tights to tie her ankles to the chair legs.

'Are you all right?' Tony asked as he saw Ylfa's eyes flicker open.

'What happened?'

'Tell me,' he said, sitting on a kitchen chair facing her. 'What are you doing here?' he said as he rolled the bloody jawbone in his hands.

'I reckoned I was going to arrest you,' she said, wincing.

'Does your head hurt?' he asked, watching a line of blood trickle down her forehead.

'Of course my head hurts,' she muttered. 'What's that?'

'It's part of next door's dog,' he said after thinking over what to say. 'Your name's Ylfa, isn't it?'

'Yes,' she said, terrified at the sight of the jawbone.

'I don't have much time, but I have something to tell you,' he said, standing up and stepping behind her.

He caught hold of Ylfa's head, pulled it back and looked down into her eyes.

60

'Where on earth is the boy?' Begga said, dusting fluff from her green satin blouse as she stood backstage where the dancers were preparing for the performance.

She had dressed in her best and the adrenaline was pumping through her. She liked to have a charged atmosphere before a show, crackling with tension, but this was too much of a good thing.

Begga had paced the floor. She flapped a hand in front of her face when she caught a sour blast of sweat, and realised it was her own.

'I know he's not the most punctual of people,' she continued. 'But this is driving me crazy.'

She peered out between the curtains over the auditorium, where guests were making their way in. She had been satisfied when the booking office had let her know how many tickets had been sold. She would have liked to have seen a few more, but ballet was certainly a branch of culture that struggled with popularity among Icelanders.

'What did you say?' she said, almost harshly, when she turned to see a grey-haired man in a suit who had appeared behind her.

'I said I'm looking for Tony,' Valdimar said. 'Is he here?'
'Well, he must be here somewhere.'
'I need a word with him.'
'You know, this isn't exactly the ideal moment,' she said,

glaring at him in exasperation. 'Are you his father, or...?'

'No,' Valdimar said with a broad smile. 'We spoke on Tuesday...'

'Yes, of course. I'm so sorry. I'm a little stressed right now. I haven't seen him...' she said, glancing around. 'But it would be best to meet up with him after the performance.'

'I'll do that,' Valdimar said, and left the stage.

Begga watched him leave and take a seat in the auditorium. 'At last,' she said, as one of the staff hurried over to her. She had sent him to Oddur's place on Grundarstígur. 'He's not home,' he panted. 'I hammered on the door again and again, but nobody answered. I couldn't see a light anywhere.'

'I don't know what to say. I hope nothing's happened to him,' she said, her voice heavy with concern, as she looked around and picked out the person she was looking for. 'You know Oddur's part pretty well, don't you?' she said shortly.

'Well, I don't know,' the dancer replied uncertainly, running his fingers through his red hair.

'Yes, you should know it. You've been with him, helping him rehearse upstairs. It's all right. I've seen you,' she smiled.

Begga had often noticed the sultry looks that passed between them when they thought nobody was looking.

'The performance is about to start,' she continued and led him by the hand to the curtain. 'And we can't let them down. Can I rely on you?' she asked earnestly as he looked out through the gap in the curtains and saw the audience.

'Excellent,' she said as the boy nodded. 'You know where the costumes are.' She clapped her hands. 'Everyone ready? Where's Tony?'

There was no answer from the dancers who were absorbed in preparing themselves, mainly as her excitable chatter went in one ear and out the other.

'Has anyone seen Tony?' she asked, hands flapping.

61

'You were wonderful,' she said, putting an arm around the shoulders of the red-haired boy who was now backstage again after having taken Oddur's part.

The performance had gone smoothly and Begga stood at the end of the stage as she watched her students receiving one round of applause after another as each scene came to an end. Her stomach lurched at the thought that she still hadn't seen Tony.

'Has anyone seen Tony? I'm so nervous,' she said, clearly worried as she cast a concerned eye over the dancers, who looked sympathetically back at her, but probably had no idea what they could contribute.

'It's going well. Four scenes to go,' said Hulda, who came over to her on tiptoe along with Davíð in their swan costumes after finishing their scene. 'No sign of Tony?' she asked when she had seen the look on Begga's face.

'No. Nothing,' she said, holding her head in her hands. 'What are we going to do? It'll be a disaster if...'

'Begga,' a voice at her side said.

'Yes?' she said, smiling quickly, as if she could expect good news as she turned to see one of the theatre staff.

'I was asked to bring you this,' he said, handing her a note. 'He said you should come up to the practice room, right away.'

'Said who?'

'Sorry. I don't know who he is.'

Begga took the note and took slow steps as she unfolded the creased scrap of paper. She stopped as she read what was written on it.

'Is everything all right, Begga?' Hulda asked.

Begga stared into space, her face as pale as if she had seen a ghost.

Without replying to Hulda, she hurried down the steps from the stage and dashed past the front row of seats and out of the door.

62

'Where's Begga?' a desperate voice demanded.

'No idea. What's going on?' Davíð said angrily, his teeth clenched. 'The whole thing's going to hell.'

The last scene but one was coming to a conclusion and the dancers backstage were in confusion as the volume of chatter swelled, each of them speaking over the next.

They looked out over the stage as the final powerful bars of the music faded out.

The audience clapped and several of the dancers made their way backstage, smiling and with arms lifted high above their heads. The arms dropped and the smiles disappeared from their faces as they saw Tony.

The planks of the stage shivered slightly at the deep sound of the kettle drums boomed through the auditorium and the almost painful tones of the violins and cellos joined in.

A low hiss came from the smoke machine as it filled the stage with a layer of mist.

Tony took slow, dignified steps from the darkness backstage to towards the three red, conical beams of light from the stage lights overhead.

He stood motionless as he entered the triangle of light at the centre of the stage and turned to face the audience.

With a slow movement, he looked down at the woman he held in his arms, then let her fall to the floor.

63

'What on earth is going on?' Begga asked in agitation as she went through the door into the practice room. She looked around and realised that the room was deserted.

'Hello?' she called out and was startled when the reply came from her office.

'Did you get my message?' the voice asked.

Begga took cautious steps to the doorway and looked into the darkened office. She saw only the dim outline of a person sitting at her desk.

'What is all this? There's a performance in progress...'

'*This script by Gunnhildur Jónsdóttir is worth consideration with a view to putting on a performance. I recommend that the writer be invited for an interview,*' the figure intoned. 'Who wrote that? The director of the theatre? The head of the dance academy?'

Begga made no reply.

'I've never been so fortunate as to be able to recall dreams,' the figure continued, sounding relaxed. 'But you, Begga. Your talent extends to a complete ballet that came to you in a dream.' The light was switched on. 'You must have known what you were doing at the time, stealing someone else's work.'

'Tony, what are you doing here?' she said, gaping at the sight of his face and body, covered in dark green and grey tones.

'Don't I look good?' he said, standing up, naked, and

twirling around. 'I know it's not exactly what your script called for. Do you mind me diverging from it?' he said with a smile.

'Please, Tony. Go,' she said, her voice quivering as she caught sight of the light of the lamp glinting on the steel points of the thimbles.

'What are you doing, Tony?'

'Or do you want the part as you... Sorry, I mean, the part as my mother wrote it?'

He stepped closer to her.

'What do you mean?'

'My mother. Gunnhildur,' he said and stood close to Begga, who failed to notice as he snatched up the jawbone from the desk.

Begga took a step back and stared at him in incomprehension.

'Tony, I don't know what you are talking about.'

'Oh,' he said with a wave of his hand. 'Yes, I think you know, deep down. Sometimes a lie can take root in a sick head,' he said, tapping at her forehead with one of the sharp points so that she squealed. 'It's almost impossible to uproot it so that the lie can be corrected. Tell the truth.'

'Tony,' she said, shaking her head as if searching for the right words.

'Are you trying, Begga? Are you covering up the lie?' he said as he swung his right hand too fast for the eye to follow across her chest. 'Don't you want to correct it?'

Begga looked down at her slashed and bloody blouse and lifted a hand to cover her breasts.

'You know, I lived for twenty years in the depths of hell because of you, Begga,' slashing with his left hand across her belly and cutting deep.

'Did you know that my mother was the devil incarnate, and that it was because of you?'

He drove all ten sharp points deep into her arms.

Begga made no sound. Her face was blank as her empty

eyes stared ahead.

'And did you know that you didn't just steal her work? You stole life itself and sucked it out of us,' he said, his voice cracking. 'Did you know that?' he wept, stooping, hands on his knees.

He took a deep breath, suddenly standing upright and raising both hands up and behind his head, sweeping them forward so that the ten blades sank into her neck.

Begga stumbled a few steps back, lost her balance and collapsed on the floor.

Tony stood over her, sank down to straddle her and leaned close to whisper in her ear.

'Did you ever dream that this moment would come? That you would finally get to meet your dragon?' he said, slipping the jawbone into his mouth, before the teeth cut deep into her throat.

64

Tony looked at Begga's bloodied corpse where he had dropped her in the centre of the stage. His head drooped and blood dripped from the jawbone. He felt like that drop of blood took a whole lifetime to reach her body.

He looked up, gazed at the audience, and saw that some of them were on their feet. He noticed a man who came slowly down the steps at the side of the rows of seats. It wasn't until he was close enough to see his face that he realised it was his grandfather. As their eyes met, Tony saw the pain shine from his face as he stood still on the steps.

The music suddenly fell silent, before the sweet tone of the oboe filled the auditorium. Tony swung his head back and looked up at the basalt columns high above in the ceiling and closed his eyes. He could see his mother by the sofa in the living room, where he stood, five years old, in the middle of the room, ready to dance.

*

'You look lovely, Tony, I'm so proud of you,' his mother said, adjusting her cream-coloured dress as she sat down.

'Thank you, Mum. Are you ready?'

'Of course I am,' she said, and her laughter tinkled as she pushed back a lock of dark hair that had fallen across her forehead. 'What part are you dancing?'

'Yours, Mum. The Dancer, of course. I'm the most famous

and best dancer in the country,' he said.

'You're sure?' she picked up the champagne glass at her side and sipped. 'You're not bored with it?'

'Mum,' he said as if he had taken offence. 'That couldn't ever happen. Ready?'

'Always.'

She smiled, her white teeth sparkled, and she made herself comfortable on the sofa.

The music began and he swept across the floor as if his feet scarcely touched the ground. His body spun like a tornado, and he leaped as gracefully as a gazelle.

He arched his back and curled into a ball on the floor, looked up and saw his mother's distorted face as she sat in the wheelchair, grey and motionless.

*

Tony straightened his back and howled with all the power in him as he stared into the auditorium and saw people standing, stunned at having witnessed this insane performance.

Did I really dance? he wondered.

He noticed Valdimar standing at the edge of the stage, his mouth hanging open as he stared at Tony.

The power of the music swelled, and Tony could feel the stage beneath his feet quiver as the kettle drums thundered a storm in his ears, and he lifted his arms high, bringing them down to slash again and again at his own body until he sank down onto one knee.

Valdimar was about to climb onto the stage, stopping short as Tony raised a hand.

'She's at home,' he gasped, blood trickling from the corner of his mouth.

'Who is?' Valdimar asked in surprise.

'Ylfa,' he said, taking the jawbone from his mouth.

'Ylfa? Home, where?'

'My mother's house,' he mumbled.

'Is she all right?'

'She will be if you're quick,' he said with a smile as he collapsed to the floor.

His grandfather climbed onto the stage and sat at Tony's side.

'What have you done, my boy?' he asked, tears flowing down his cheeks.

'It's all right, Grandad. I'll be fine,' he said, his voice fading, and shut his eyes. 'I've lived life as a dead man. Now all I want is to die.'

'My poor boy. Forgive me, my darling boy,' Jón said, wrapping his arms around Tony.

'It would have been fun to breathe fire as well, wouldn't it, Grandad?' Tony whispered, looking up through half-closed eyes.

'What do you mean?' he said, looking into his eyes. 'Like a real dragon.'

He took a deep breath.

He breathed no more.

65

Valdimar burst into the house.

'Ylfa? Are you here?' he called out several times, checking every room. He put a hand to his chest as he felt a stab of pain and his determination to find Ylfa was magnified when he saw Gunnhildur in the living room.

Valdimar looked up the parquet-laid stairs to the upper floor. He went up the steps and into a dark corridor where there were four closed doors.

The first one opened onto a sea of cardboard boxes that filled the room. There was nothing to see in the next two. He saw Ylfa as he opened the fourth door and switched on the light.

She was tied to a chair, facing a television that was showing an old video recording.

Valdimar hurried over to her and ripped off the tape that covered her mouth.

'Are you all right?' he demanded, as he looked at her face, puffed with weeping, leaving rivulets of make-up down her cheeks.

Ylfa said nothing, but stared at the screen.

'Ylfa...?'

'This boy has been through hell,' she whispered.

Valdimar turned to the screen. The man behind the camera chuckled constantly, mumbling to himself in a slurred voice. He pointed the camera at three drunk individuals who sat on the sofa and clinked glasses for the camera. The table in front of them was packed with bottles and glasses, and a cigarette smouldered in an ashtray.

The face of the woman wearing nothing but underwear as she sat between two men was familiar and Valdimar couldn't be sure of Gunnhildur's age, but she had been considerably younger when the video had been recorded.

'Dance, my darling,' she slurred. 'Show the gentlemen what your mother has taught you.'

The camera focused on Tony, who could hardly have been more than five years old.

'Aren't you going to dance?' asked one of the men on the sofa, and as the camera zoomed in on him, it could be seen that he had pulled aside one of the cups of Gunnhildur's bra so that he could squeeze and fondle a breast.

Gunnhildur groaned, and then quickly sat up straight. 'Dance, boy!' she screeched.

The lens lingered on Tony as he looked in terror from her to the camera and back. His lips trembled and a flood of urine appeared at his feet.

He looked down for a long moment, before lifting his hands high over his head and turning in circles. The camera zoomed in on his feet. Blood seeped through the bindings and down to the ballet shoes tightly laced to his feet.

Valdimar switched off the television.

As he loosened the tights that bound Ylfa's hands and feet to the chair, he looked around at the chaos in the room. Seven or eight pictures of Tony and his mother hung on the walls, all of them tilted at wild angles, the glass broken. A bookcase had been tipped over, a desk lay on its side and the mattress on the bed had been slashed into two. Valdimar felt that he could hear the howls of the maddened person who had wrecked the room.

*

'That was quite an opening night,' Ylfa said as she

listened to Valdimar's account, sitting on the steps by the front door.

'It certainly was,' he said, his eyes on the street light and the fine particles of snow that glittered as they fell to earth through the cone of brightness. 'I thought...' he said, then paused.

'Thought what?'

'I was sure that he had done you some real harm.'

'You don't get rid of me that easily,' she said, jabbing him with her elbow. 'I thought the same. I made a desperate attempt to appeal to his sympathetic side, and told him all about the problems between me and Steinthór. Maybe that worked, because that was when he dragged me upstairs and put that video on.' She massaged the sore patches on her wrists where the bindings had cut deep. 'How can anyone complain after that? You saw just a fraction of what that boy went through, Valdimar. Anyway, what time is it?'

Valdimar glanced at his watch.

'Almost midnight,' he said, and Ylfa sighed. 'Something wrong?'

'No. Well, I don't know. I didn't get a chance to call her.'

'Who?'

'My little girl,' she said thoughtfully.

'All the things we see and hear shouldn't allow us to be any less concerned about ourselves, Ylfa. You can speak to her tomorrow,' he said, trying to sound buoyant. 'Aren't you hungry? How about you come with me and get something to eat? I'm sure Ásta will have something in the microwave at home.'

'She killed him.'

'She, who?' he asked.

'Gunnhildur. She killed John. He came to see them. When he saw the state of the place, he was furious with Tony. They argued furiously and Tony stormed out. When he came back, John was dead on the kitchen floor and

Gunnhildur sat there with a carving knife in her hand. Tony never got out of her what actually happened.'

'I see,' Valdimar said, and his gaze went back to watching the flakes of falling snow.

'Do you expect either of us will ever get to investigate a case again after all this?'

'Why?' he asked in surprise.

'We don't come out of this covered in glory.'

'Ylfa, sometimes things can look extremely complex. But that's rarely the way it is. This time the solution was too obvious,' he said as she sniffed, and he handed her a handkerchief. 'Maybe what we were missing was the one mathematical coincidence that would have made the puzzle come together,' he continued, and gave her a jab of his own with an elbow.

'Yes, maybe,' she said, and watched a cat that stalked along the pavement towards them.

It rubbed against their legs, miaowed, and went in through the door of the house.